SHAWNA DELACORTE

WHO'S BEEN SLEEPING IN MY BED?

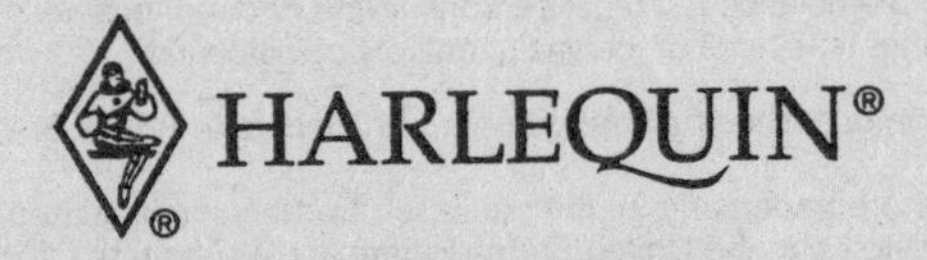

TORONTO • NEW YORK • LONDON
AMSTERDAM • PARIS • SYDNEY • HAMBURG
STOCKHOLM • ATHENS • TOKYO • MILAN • MADRID
PRAGUE • WARSAW • BUDAPEST • AUCKLAND

ISBN-13: 978-0-373-69246-0
ISBN-10: 0-373-69246-3

WHO'S BEEN SLEEPING IN MY BED?

This edition published by arrangement with Harlequin Books S.A.

www.eHarlequin.com

Printed in U.S.A.

Everything seemed to be in order, except for the woman asleep in his cabin.

Reece took in everything about the stranger—the wet clothes clinging to her body, the tousled, short blond hair and a beautiful face that even in sleep was in obvious turmoil. He felt a definite tug on his reality, a strange combination of lust and concern.

Should he wake her and demand to know what she was doing in his cabin? He spotted her purse on the end table. As he reached for it she stirred, then jerked to attention.

Her eyes went wide with fright as her gaze landed on him.

Her voice was anything but firm as she eased her way out of the chair. She moved behind it in an obvious attempt to put a barricade between them. "Who...who are you?"

"Well, Goldilocks…this is my cabin, and I want to know why you've been sleeping in my bed."

ABOUT THE AUTHOR

Although award-winning author Shawna Delacorte has lived most of her life in Los Angeles and has a background working in television production, she is currently living in Wichita, Kansas. Among her writing accomplishments she is honored to include her placement on the *USA TODAY* bestseller list. In addition to writing full-time, she teaches a fiction writing class in the Division of Continuing Education at Wichita State University. Shawna enjoys hearing from her readers and can be reached at 6505 E. Central, Box #300, Wichita, KS 67206. You may also visit her at her author page at the Harlequin Web site: www.eHarlequin.com.

Books by Shawna Delacorte

HARLEQUIN INTRIGUE

413—LOVER UNKNOWN
520—SECRET LOVER
656—IN HIS SAFEKEEPING
846—THE SEDGWICK CURSE
979—WHO'S BEEN SLEEPING IN MY BED?

CAST OF CHARACTERS

Brandi Doyle—Why would someone stalk this quiet, unassuming woman? And worse yet, why would someone abduct her?

Reece Covington—He's hiding away from society in his mountain cabin after serving a prison term for something he didn't do. After his last experience, will he allow himself to be drawn in by another woman who claims to need his help?

Lt. Frank James—Good cop gone bad or simply overzealous in his duties?

Lyle Hanover—Assistant D.A. who prosecuted Reece based on Lt. James's testimony. Should he have looked at the case a little closer?

Joe Hodges—Is this FBI agent the friend he pretends to be, or does he have an agenda of his own?

Chapter One

Brandi Doyle glanced back over her shoulder. Panic surged through her body, a panic driven by fear. The rain pelted against her face, stinging her skin. Had she managed to elude her pursuer? The stalker everyone kept telling her didn't exist? The person who was only a figment of her imagination?

The very real man who just a few hours ago had abducted her?

She dug her shoes into the slippery mud as she fought to maintain her footing in the drenching downpour. Her heart pounded. Her chest heaved with each gulp of air she sucked into her lungs, but she didn't dare slow down.

It seemed as if it had been hours since she'd managed to escape from her abductor's car when he'd stopped for gas at the small service station on the mountain road—hours that she had been running through the woods. But a quick glance at her watch told her it had only been thirty minutes. Intellectually, she knew the rain would obscure any trace of her tracks, but she couldn't shake the feeling that her abductor was only a few feet behind her and closing in.

She headed in the direction where she thought the lake and some cabins were, a place where she might be able to get some help. It was an area where she had done a lot of photography. If only she could be sure of her exact location. If only she hadn't been blindfolded. A shiver rippled through her body, part anxiety and part chill. She was soaked to the skin without even a jacket to provide a modicum of warmth.

It would be dark soon and she needed to find some sort of shelter. She forced herself onward, ignoring the ache in her legs. She had to put as much distance as she could between her and her abductor—and as quickly as possible.

Another hundred feet she came to a fire road. She ran parallel to the road, staying in the woods, hidden from view. Shrubbery attacked her legs and arms. Bushes scratched her face and hands, but she knew she didn't dare venture out into the open—she didn't dare expose herself to her abductor.

Then she spotted it through the trees—a cabin at the edge of the fire road. A little tremor of excitement tried to take hold. It was the off season, too early for summer vacationers. There was a good chance the cabin would be vacant. It would provide her shelter from the storm, a means of hiding from her pursuer and a place to gather her thoughts and make a plan of action.

The carport was empty—a good sign. She knocked on the door and received no response. She tried the door but found it locked. She circled the cabin, checking the windows until she found an unlocked one that opened into the kitchen. Once inside, she breathed a sigh of relief. She was out of the wind and rain and no longer visible to anyone looking for her.

Brandi took a quick look around, making sure the cabin was empty. It was—for the moment. The rumpled sheets and blanket on the unmade bed in the bedroom left her with an uneasy feeling. She paused in the bathroom long enough to towel-dry her dripping wet hair. She studied her face in the mirror. The scratches weren't too bad, but they needed to be cleaned. She washed her face, then found some antiseptic in a bathroom cupboard.

She returned to the kitchen. The refrigerator was mostly empty—nothing perishable, such as fresh meat, vegetables or even a quart of orange juice. Hopefully the owner only used the cabin on weekends in spite of the evidence of the unmade bed. The shelves contained canned goods. She opened a can of soup. It wasn't much, but it eased her hunger pangs.

Her guilt, however, wasn't as easily appeased. She had broken into someone's cabin and stolen food. Not a very admirable thing to do, even though it had been necessary. Her fears quickly overruled her guilt.

She made a quick trip through the cabin again, looking out each of the windows. She satisfied herself that she had not been followed, that there wasn't anyone lurking outside. She also noticed that there wasn't a phone. She slumped into a large, comfortable chair. For the first time in several hours she drew in an easy breath. She pulled the strap from across her chest and over her head, then set the small, attached purse on the end table. She had been wearing the purse when her abductor had grabbed her, and she had managed to hang on to it—an almost involuntary action of clinging to something she owned.

She needed to think, to make sense of what had happened, to figure out what to do next. Her eyelids grew heavy. She could not fight off the exhaustion, as much emotional as it was physical. A moment later darkness descended around her, and she slipped into an uneasy sleep.

REECE COVINGTON PULLED HIS four-wheel-drive SUV off the fire road, parking in the carport attached to his cabin. He had intended to enclose the carport, making it a garage and cutting a door from the garage directly into the cabin. Stormy days like today made him wish he had finished the project.

He dashed through the rain to the covered front porch while juggling a sack of groceries. He had been hiding out in his cabin in the Cascade Mountains for three months, ever since his release from prison. Two years of his life taken away from him for something he didn't do. Two years spent building up resentment toward the woman who had set him up and the rogue cop who had framed him.

He unlocked the door and stepped inside, then came to an abrupt halt. His heart jumped a beat and his senses went on full alert as his experienced gaze made a quick yet expert sweep of the room. Everything seemed to be in order, everything where it belonged.

Everything except for the woman asleep in the chair.

He moved quietly to the kitchen, searching for

anything that looked out of place. He spotted the window where she had entered. He noted the empty soup can. He set the bag of groceries in the refrigerator, then moved stealthily toward the bedroom. He did not want to wake the intruder nor did he want to alert anyone else who might be with her.

He made a quick search of the bedroom. It was exactly the way he left it. So was the bathroom, except for the wet washcloth, the towel and the bottle of antiseptic on the counter.

He returned to the living room. He took in everything about the stranger—the wet clothes clinging to her body, her muddy shoes, the tousled, short blond hair and the beautiful face with the numerous scratches. A face that even in sleep was covered in turmoil. He felt a definite tug on his reality, a strange combination of lust and concern. He steeled himself against the unwanted and unexpected feelings—both of them.

He had been down that path before with a beautiful stranger who had claimed to need his help. It had ended up costing him two years of his life and his career. And before that there was his travesty of an engagement to a woman who had jilted him at the altar and gone back to her former boyfriend.

Yes, indeed. It would be a cold day in hell before he made the mistake of being suckered in by another beautiful woman, no matter how vulnerable she appeared to be or how much she professed to need his help.

He continued to stare at the stranger as he turned the situation over in his mind. She didn't seem to pose an immediate threat to him. Should he wake her and demand to know what she was doing in his cabin or wait until she woke on her own? He spotted her purse on the end table. As he reached for it she stirred, opened her eyes, then jerked to attention.

Her eyes went wide with fright as her gaze landed on him.

Her voice was anything but firm as she eased her way out of the chair. She moved behind it in an obvious attempt to put a barricade between them. "Who…who are you? What are you doing here?"

His reply was succinct, his voice carrying all the authority of someone in charge. "Well, Goldilocks…I'm Papa Bear and this is my cabin. I want to know why you've been eating my soup and sleeping in my chair." He raked his gaze slowly over the obviously frightened woman, but was totally unprepared for her next move.

She bolted for the door of the cabin and ran blindly out into the rain, fear propelling her every step. Reece followed close on her heels, catching up with her about ten feet from the porch. He picked her up and threw her over his shoulder in a fireman's carry. She struggled, twisting and turning in an attempt to get loose. His tight hold thwarted her attempts to free herself from his control.

"Lady…calm down. I'm not going to hurt you. I'm bigger than you are. I'm stronger than you. I don't like being out here in the mud and rain. Stop struggling because whether you like it or not, we're going back inside. You're going to tell me who you are and why you broke into my cabin."

She pounded her fists against his back. "You put me

down this second." Even to her own ears her demands sounded weak and ineffectual. Her mind raced, darting frantically from one fear to another as he carried her inside the cabin. Panic continued to rampage through her body, totally wiping out any logic that might have been tenaciously clinging to her reality. The moment he set her down, she dashed for the door again.

With a speed that truly shocked her, he lunged forward and tackled her around the waist. In one smooth motion he shoved her to the floor and pinned her down with his body.

She had never been as frightened as she was at that moment, not even when her abductor had grabbed her. The bitter taste of adrenaline filled her mouth. Her heart pounded wildly, pushing her fear to every part of her body. Her throat threatened to close. She swallowed several times, but it did nothing to stop the sick churning in the pit of her stomach. It felt as if all the oxygen had been sucked out of the air. She gasped for breath. She lashed out at him in panic, scratching the side of his face.

"Damn!" He grabbed both her wrists and held them above her head. "Settle down, you little hellcat. I told you I'm not going to hurt you. Now, calm down. Will you stay put and stop struggling if I let go of your wrists?"

The tears welled in her eyes. She tried to blink them away. A sob caught in her throat. She barely managed to force out the words. "Please don't hurt me."

His breathing quickened as he continued to struggle with her. She was obviously very frightened, but he also knew that she was hysterical and in danger of injuring herself if she tried to run again. He could not let her up from the floor before she regained control of her emotions. He forced a calm to his voice, one he didn't feel but one he hoped would have an effect on her.

"I told you, I'm not going to hurt you." He held both of her wrists in one of his hands and with the other one he grabbed both sides of her jaw and held her head still. He fixed her with a steady gaze. "Listen to me. I'm not going to hurt you. Do you hear me? Are you listening to me? Answer me."

He saw her eyes focus on him. They were still filled with fear, but he knew he finally had her attention. He dropped his voice to what he hoped was a soothing level. "Quiet down. Be still. I'm not going to hurt you. Do you understand me?"

She nodded her head.

"Say it. I want to hear the words. Do you understand what I'm saying? I'm not going to hurt you."

Her voice trembled, but the words finally came out. "I...I hear you."

"Okay. Now, take a deep breath, then another one. You're going to be all right. Take another breath." He felt some of the tension drain from her body as her muscles relaxed a bit. When her breathing smoothed out until it was steady, he let go of her face. "I'm going to turn your wrists loose now, then we'll get up from the floor. I want you to sit on the sofa. Do you understand?"

She took a deep breath. Her voice still contained a

slight quaver as she spoke, but she had better control of it. "Yes."

His face was so close to hers that he could feel her breath against his skin. Even disheveled, dirty and scratched, she still radiated a beauty and desirability that pushed his testosterone to the limit. And having his body on top of hers definitely aggravated the awkward situation. He had to break the physical contact before she had a valid reason to be concerned about what could happen.

He cautiously released her wrists from his grasp and allowed her to slowly lower her arms. "I'm going to stand up now. Are you sure you're calm and in control of your emotions?" He felt a little more of her tension drain away. He rose to his feet, then held out his hand to help her up from the floor. She hesitated, then cautiously accepted his assistance.

To her surprise, her fear level didn't elevate when he grasped her hand. He certainly radiated a commanding presence, but she had picked up on something else about him. His blue eyes had been wary as he stared at her, rather than menacing. They were honest and seemed to take in everything that was going on. Now that she was in control of herself again, she realized that there wasn't anything potentially hurtful radiating from him.

Was it just wishful thinking on her part? Hoping she hadn't become ensnared in even more trouble than she had been in a few hours earlier? Hoping she hadn't stumbled into the hideout of a crazed rapist or a serial killer? She knew he wasn't the man who had abducted her, but could he be in league with her stalker?

Her throat tightened and a sick feeling churned in the pit of her stomach again. Was she about to meet her final doom?

He guided her to the sofa in front of the fireplace. "I'm not going to hurt you. Now sit down and stay put while I build a fire and get some heat in here." He started to reach for some logs, then turned his gaze on her again. He told her what she intellectually knew, but had not emotionally accepted.

"You can't wander around in the rain. Besides, it will be dark soon. All you'll accomplish is getting yourself hurt." He returned his attention to starting a fire.

The cold, the wet and the emotional turmoil finally caught up with her. She shivered in hard spasms. She reached for the blanket folded across the back of the sofa and pulled it around her. Was she now a prisoner of this man? What should she do?

What *could* she do?

She studied him as he placed a couple of logs in the fireplace, then lit the small pieces of kindling. He looked as if he hadn't shaved for a couple of days, but it didn't do anything to hide his handsome features. His wet hair lay matted against his head, dark tendrils brushing against the top of his jacket collar. She noted his broad shoulders and long legs. He appeared to be in his late thirties. Most certainly a very sexy man with a magnetic aura and definite appeal.

She closed her eyes for a moment as she shook the thoughts from her head. She had been stalked, then abducted. She had escaped into the woods in an attempt to elude her pursuer. She had been running for her life—literally. And now she was trapped in a mountain cabin with this stranger who had clearly demonstrated how indefensible her position was when he had tossed her over his shoulder as if she were nothing more than a sack of feathers and hauled her back inside, then had physically held her against her will.

Any thoughts about the desirability of this man were not only totally inappropriate, they were absurd.

Reece's voice broke into her thoughts as he closed the screen in front of the fire. "There—that should take the chill out of the air and help you warm up."

He wasn't sure what to do now. She sat huddled in the corner of the sofa with the blanket wrapped around her. Another hard jolt of lust struck him, tempered by the realization of how frightened and vulnerable she appeared. It had been two years and three months since he had been this close to a desirable woman. The sight played on his emotions and tugged at his senses. He tried to shove away the feelings. He went to the kitchen, took the sack from the grocery store out of the refrigerator and put everything away where it belonged, hoping the activity would give him time to think.

A few minutes later he returned to the living room. She was exactly where he had left her, scrunched in the corner of the sofa. He swallowed his discomfort and uneasiness as he forced an outer calm.

"Well, Goldilocks...are you sufficiently recovered enough to talk to me? Do you have a name?"

She pulled up all the courage she could muster as she attempted to project a commanding attitude. "Do you?"

"No you don't, Goldilocks. It's my cabin. You're the trespasser. I'm the one who has the right to ask questions and demand answers."

She glared at him. "Stop calling me Goldilocks!"

He suppressed the wry grin that tugged at the corners of his mouth. She had spirit. Even as frightened as she obviously was—as frightened as anyone would be under the circumstances—she had managed to put forth some heated sparks of independence. He found that very appealing. He had never been particularly interested in the clinging-vine type of woman nor the type who constantly needed to have her ego fed—not even as the occasional one-night stand.

He made eye contact with her and held it for a long moment before speaking. "Then tell me what to call you."

Her emotions had been stretched, punched and pulled so taut that she didn't have anything left other than the underlying current of fear that continued to run just below the surface. "Brandi..." She broke the eye contact as she quickly looked away. "Brandi Doyle."

"Well, Brandi Doyle, what are you doing in my cabin?" The question left him uneasy. Was her obvious vulnerability getting to him? Was he allowing himself to be drawn into yet another bad situation with a woman where he would end up regretting that he hadn't just allowed her to escape into the storm and out of his life?

"I...I needed someplace where I could get out of the storm."

"I didn't see a car. How did you get here? Why were you wandering around in the storm? Where did you come from?" He reached out and almost touched her face, withdrawing his hand before he made physical contact. "And where did you get those scratches on your face?"

"I—" This was no good. She didn't have a clue who he was, other than the owner of the cabin. Or so he claimed.

True…even though she didn't have any means of protecting herself, he hadn't done anything other than bring her back inside from the storm. True…he had released her unharmed, as he'd said he would. True…he just might be an honorable and trustworthy man.

But could she really trust him with the truth about how and why she happened to be in his cabin?

She drew in a steadying breath in an effort to calm her galloping anxiety and ease her trepidation. She chose her words with great care. "I apologize for being here. I had no right to break into your cabin." She rose to her feet and dropped the blanket on the sofa. "I'll leave so you can go about your business." She picked up her purse, screwed up her courage and headed toward the door.

Reece grabbed her arm and with his other hand took the purse from her. "Wait a minute. You can't go wandering in the woods with a storm raging around you. Besides—" he glanced toward the window "—in another ten minutes it will be dark outside."

He eyed her carefully, maintaining his hold on her as she tried to wrest her arm from his grip. "Are you in some kind of trouble? Are you in danger? Was my cabin more of a place for you to hide than merely somewhere to get out of the rain?"

Her words came out almost as a whisper, her voice pleading. "Please…let go of me. I want to leave."

The quaver in her voice answered his questions, and the obvious fear that emanated from the depths of her eyes confirmed those answers. And it also told him that hell must have frozen over while he wasn't looking. He had just been suckered into helping yet another beautiful woman in distress. Would he live to regret it this time, too?

She looked up at him, this time holding the eye contact. He saw the confusion in her troubled hazel eyes. He loosened his grip on her arm and guided her back to the sofa. He softened his voice, hoping it would instill some confidence and allay her concerns and obvious fears.

"Sit down." He opened her purse and took out her driver's license. "So, your name really is Brandi." He noted her address in Rocky Shores, Washington—a city of about thirty thousand people in the greater Seattle metropolitan area. *Rocky Shores*…he turned that interesting tidbit of information over in his mind as he handed everything back to her.

He perched on the arm of the sofa and studied her for a moment. "Tell me what's going on…please."

She hesitated as if she wasn't sure what to do or what to say. She emitted a sigh of resignation as she slumped back and allowed her tensed muscles to relax a little bit. He didn't seem as threatening as he had earlier. True to his word, he had not harmed her. A lot of the fear had drained from her reality—but not all of it. "I don't even know who you are. Why would you want to hear about my problems?"

"Fair enough question. My name is Reece Covington. You're obviously in some kind of trouble and by breaking into my cabin you've involved me in it even if that wasn't your intention." Was he about to repeat the same colossal mistake that had landed him in prison for two years? He took a deep breath, held it for a moment, then slowly exhaled. He was not at all sure he was doing the right thing. His words came out slowly, surrounded by a touch of the uncertainty that jittered inside him.

"Perhaps there's something I can do to help you."

"How could you help me?"

"I don't know. First, you'll have to tell me what the problem is, then we'll see if there's some way I can help. It could be that the only thing I can do is provide you with a ride back to Rocky Shores." He flashed an engaging smile, one he hoped would instill a feeling of confidence. "But that would certainly be better than walking back."

All the defiance drained out of her body, to be replaced with despair. She didn't know what to do or what to say. Her words were barely above a whisper, a very frightened whisper. "No one can help. No one believes me."

He moved off the arm of the sofa and sat down next to her. "What is it that no one believes?" He was digging the hole deeper and deeper. He was becoming too involved in something that was none of his business—something that could only cause him more trouble than he wanted to accept. More trouble than he needed, especially now.

"All right." She screwed up her determination. "You asked and here it is. For the past month someone has been stalking me."

It was the last thing he had expected her to say, but it grabbed his attention. He could tell by the expression on her face that she was serious. "Stalking you? In what way?"

"Well…sometimes it was just a feeling that someone was watching me when I would be out at various places. Things like following me around the grocery store. I would turn around and look, but didn't see anyone I recognized or even anyone who seemed to be paying any attention to me. At night I would sometimes hear sounds outside my house as if someone was checking to see if any of the doors or windows were unlocked. My phone would ring. I could hear breathing, but no one would answer me. It wasn't the type of heavy breathing that you would think of as an obscene call, just someone on the line who didn't say anything."

"Well, that could have just been your imagination. Or maybe kids playing a prank."

"That's what the police said when I tried to report it. They didn't believe me." A frown wrinkled across her forehead, an angry frown that matched her tone of voice. "In fact, they were very condescending. They implied that I was nothing more than some hysterical neurotic female with an overactive imagination who should take a tranquilizer and get some rest."

A little snort of disgust escaped his throat before he could stop it. "In my experience, that's typical of the way the Rocky Shores Police Department handles things."

"There's more. There was a voice—a strange, unreal type of voice—that would reach out to me."

"What do you mean by strange and unreal? Was it a man's voice or a woman's? What was different about this voice?"

"I'm not sure. It was sort of...well, like it was mechanical or something like that. It was a man's voice."

"Do you mean like a computer-generated voice? Something like that?"

The light of recognition came into her eyes. "Yes! That's it. A computer-generated voice, not a real person."

"You said it reached out to you. What do you mean? How did it *reach out* to you?"

Brandi scrunched up her face as she tried to come up with the right words to explain something that didn't have any rational explanation. "It was as if it materialized out of thin air when there was no one around, at least no one I could see. Once it was in the fog during the day. Another time it was at night."

"What did this voice say?"

"It called my name and told me to be careful, that it was coming for me. There were a couple of occasions when I could tell that someone had been in my house. Nothing was missing and everything appeared to be in the right place, but I could tell someone had looked through my things."

"Your *things*...what kind of things? Do you mean like some pervert pawing through your underwear?"

"No. It seemed to be my office and my darkroom."

Reece cocked his head and raised an eyebrow. "Your

office? Your darkroom? You work from home? Are you a professional photographer or is it just a hobby?"

"It's what I do for a living. Mostly weddings and portraits, but I'm also working on a coffee-table-type book—scenic photographs depicting the unique and beautiful sights of Washington."

A sudden thought struck her, one that triggered a moment of anxiety. She tried to shove down the apprehension as she stared at him with a skeptical eye. She wasn't sure she should open a can of worms by asking the question or, for that matter, whether she really wanted to know the answer.

"You sound like a policeman who's interrogating a suspect. Are you…uh, are you a policeman?" The apprehension churned inside her. She held her breath as she waited for his response. Under normal circumstances a policeman would be a blessing and a relief, but not this time. Not now. Not with what she had seen when—

"Me? A policeman?" If the thought hadn't been so preposterous it might have been funny. "No, I'm not a policeman." A level of caution pushed to the forefront. Something about the way she had asked the question caught his attention. It was almost as if she was afraid he might be a policeman rather than hoping he was one.

The more she talked, the more he became fascinated with the tale she had to tell. He had dealt with this type of situation before. As a highly paid, very successful private investigator, he had handled several stalking cases during his career.

Career. He almost laughed out loud at the word, a

laugh of bitter resentment. His extremely profitable career had been flushed down the toilet along with two years of his life when he was wrongly convicted and sent to prison. Now, he had enough money socked away from before his arrest to sustain him for a while, plus the profits from selling his house.

And he had the cabin. He had bought it eight years ago and had taken great pains to conceal its ownership—just as he had the ownership of his SUV—by using a series of dummy corporations and other evasive tactics. At the time he'd purchased it, the cabin's purpose had been to provide a haven for clients who needed protection and a secure place to hide witnesses for a high-powered defense attorney who had regularly engaged his services. But now his needs were the most basic, and his expenses almost nonexistent.

And here was Brandi Doyle threatening that anonymity. If he had any sense at all he would drive her back to town, drop her off at her house and forget that she had ever crossed his path.

"So what does all of this lead up to? What happened today that you ended up in my cabin in the mountains in a rainstorm?" He saw the discomfort in her body language and the wariness in her eyes. Once again she had managed to touch a spot deep inside him that he had tried to protect against the vulnerability she couldn't hide.

Brandi stared at the flames in the fireplace. She had already said too much, given more information to this complete stranger than she should have. Had she put herself in additional danger, more than what already pursued her? She wished she had some answers, but all she had were questions.

Questions and fears.

Her voice rang hollow. She couldn't keep her emotional pain tucked away as she spoke. At least he was listening—or maybe just pretending to listen. Either way, it was more credence than the police had given her when she'd tried to report her stalker.

"Today someone abducted me as I was about to get into my car to go to the grocery store. I managed to escape when he stopped for gas. I ran into the woods and kept running until I saw your cabin."

It was the last thing he had expected her to say and one more detail that added to his growing interest in her story. He fought to keep it on a purely intellectual level while attempting to ignore her physical attributes and the vulnerability that continued to reach out to him.

He maintained his outer composure, making sure he didn't show her any of his thoughts or feelings. "Do you know who abducted you? Or why?"

"I have no idea why anyone would want to abduct me. I'm not wealthy. My family isn't wealthy. I don't have an ex-husband or even a spurned lover who would be wanting to get back at me for some real or imagined deed. I lead a basically uneventful life. I don't have any enemies that I'm aware of. I'm at a complete loss as to why this is happening to me."

She paused and took in a calming breath before continuing. "I guess I can't blame the police for not believing me. I know everything I've said sounds absurd. And to make things worse, I think...uh, I think the man who abducted me was…" Once again she drew in a deep breath in an effort to still her rattled nerves. She stared at the burning logs, her words a mere whisper.

"I think he was a policeman."

Chapter Two

Reece's senses jumped to rigid attention as he rose to his feet and stood facing Brandi. "You were abducted by a policeman?" His words came machine-gun fast as the excitement raced through him. "Are you sure? How do you know he was a policeman? Was he in uniform? Do you know his name? What did he look like? How old was he? Had you ever seen him before?"

Had he heard her correctly? It was a rogue cop who had framed *him* for a crime he didn't commit. A quick surge of anger jolted through him. He would never be able to get those two years back, but he was determined to get the people responsible for sending him to prison. It was all he had thought about for the entire two years. Was it even remotely possible that what happened to him could somehow be connected to her predicament?

His office had been in Rocky Shores. It had been a detective with the Rocky Shores Police Department who had framed him. *She* lived in Rocky Shores. Could it be the same cop? If it had happened in Seattle, or some other large city, he would have said it was preposterous—too coincidental to be real. But in Rocky

Shores—a city of only thirty thousand people? Or was he desperately grasping at straws in an attempt to connect the two incidents?

He repeated his question, determined to get an answer that satisfied him. He leaned forward, his hands on the back of the sofa on each side of her head—his face almost touching hers. He slowly repeated the question, clearly enunciating each word in a low voice that left no room for any confusion concerning his seriousness and demand for an answer.

"How do you know he was a policeman?"

Brandi stared at Reece in several seconds of stunned silence. He had suddenly come alive, catching her totally off guard. The intensity etched on his features matched the resolve in the depth of his blue eyes. His commanding presence was unnervingly close, his face so near that she could literally feel the strength of his determination radiate to her.

And that wasn't all. His clean, masculine scent was as sexy and appealing as if he had just splashed himself with an aphrodisiac guaranteed to work its wonders on unsuspecting women. It was the type of thing that could make the strongest will melt on the spot. She suspected that if they continued in such close proximity she would succumb with very little objection in spite of the earlier frightening physical encounter.

She tried to douse the flame of desire he had ignited inside her—the totally inappropriate desire—by forcing her attention back to the reality of the present and the danger that had suddenly invaded her life. Something was going on. Something more than the owner of this cabin wanting to know why she had trespassed on his property. He already knew a lot about her, but the only thing she knew about him was his name.

If that was really his name.

It left her with a very uncomfortable feeling. He had blatantly displayed how physically vulnerable she was when he had thrown her over his shoulder as if she were nothing more than a sack of feathers and then pinned her to the floor when she had tried to run again. With each ensuing question her emotional vulnerability increased.

And she didn't like the sensation—the same helplessness that had beset her for the past month. An emotional upheaval that she couldn't control.

Somehow, she had to regain the upper hand over what was happening. She had to once again be in charge of her own life. Whether anyone believed her or not, she knew she was in danger, and it was up to her to protect herself from the unknown person who seemed determined to harm her. She had tried to go to the police and had been dismissed as if she was some delusional nut case—some *irrational woman.* She didn't have anyone she could count on other than herself.

His voice interrupted her attempt to make sense of things. "You haven't answered my question, Brandi. How do you know the man who abducted you was a police officer?"

She steeled her determination, put her hands on his hard, muscled chest and pushed him away. "Stop browbeating me!"

He straightened up as her words sank in. And along

with his realization of what she had said was the heated sensation of her hands against his chest. One thing was blatantly clear. He had to avoid any more physical contact with her. Two years in prison followed by three months of self-imposed isolation had left him with a very tenuous hold on his libido. Being around her had ignited a burning need that all the cold showers in the world would not be able to quench.

He took a step backward. "I'm sorry. I didn't mean to make you uncomfortable. It's just that I'm very interested in what you're saying. I want to know about this man you claim abducted you. I...uh...I know some of the members of the Rocky Shores police force—"

"You're friends with the police?"

He saw the alarm register on her features and knew he had said the wrong thing. "No, I didn't say I was friends with any of the members of the Rocky Shores Police Department. I merely said I knew some of them. I came in contact with several of the boys in blue over the years. Sort of an occupational hazard."

"Occupational hazard?" She furrowed her brow in confusion. "What is it you do?"

"I was a private investigator." He clenched his jaw in a hard line of determination. "And a damn good one, too. I lived on Mercer Island, but my office was in Rocky Shores."

"A private investigator?" Her entire demeanor brightened. "I had considered hiring a private investigator when the police wouldn't help me with my stalker."

"Why didn't you?"

A downcast expression crossed her face. "I guess I

thought it would all come to a stop by itself, the same way it had started. I kept putting it off—" she emitted a sigh of resignation "—and then it was too late. Maybe if I'd hired a private investigator I wouldn't be in this mess now."

"So, let me try this for the third time." His words and tone of voice were part exasperation and part determination. "How do you know the man who abducted you was a police officer?"

"Well...he was dressed in plainclothes, but when he grabbed me his jacket came open and I saw a badge clipped to his belt." She saw Reece's eyes narrow as if he was turning the information over in his mind. A little tremor of anxiety fluttered around inside her. Had she said the wrong thing?

"Describe him for me."

"I only got a glimpse of him before he blindfolded me."

"Do the best you can. Let's start with his size. How tall do you think he was? My size? Shorter? Taller? Heavier? Lighter? What was your impression of his physical presence?"

She looked at him quizzically. "Why do you want to know? Why are you suddenly so interested?" She returned her gaze to the flames crackling in the fireplace. She had to admit that she felt a little more at ease around him. Whatever fears she might have harbored about Reece Covington and her safety while in his cabin had subsided. If he had wanted to harm her there was nothing preventing him from having already done it. He had her in his control and hadn't taken advantage of the situation.

"No one believed me before I was abducted, including the police. I know no one will believe me now, especially the police, if I say that I think it was one of their own who did it."

"I'm not everyone else. I'm me and I'm interested—*very* interested."

He searched the depth of her eyes and once again felt the emotional tug of her vulnerability, something he didn't want to experience or even know about. He also felt the physical pull on his desires, something he most assuredly wanted to explore even though he knew he shouldn't. But a very real sensation all the same.

"Why? Why would you be interested in what happened?" A shortness of breath caught in her lungs. He seemed to be looking into the very depths of her soul. If she thought she had been in trouble while running through the woods to escape her abductor and again when Reece had tackled her, she didn't know what to call what was happening now. She had run for her life and ended up in a cabin with a man who left her confused, unnerved and uneasy. But she was no longer fearful of his presence.

Quite the contrary. In some strange way she felt a sensual pull toward him, a totally inappropriate attraction. There was something very solid and real about this man, something very reassuring. He exuded a silent strength that said he knew who he was and could handle himself in any type of situation, whether physical or mental.

And he claimed to be a private investigator. Perhaps he was just what she needed. Could it be that fate had delivered her into the hands of someone who would believe her story? Someone who could actually help her find her way out of the nightmare?

Reece shifted his weight from one foot to the other in a moment of discomfort as he turned her words over in his mind. "Let's just say that I have an old score to settle with someone."

He allowed his tensed muscles to relax while carefully choosing his words. He didn't want to do or say anything that would cause her to stop confiding in him. "I want to find out if there's a possible connection between what's been happening to you and something from my past."

"What are you talking about?"

"I don't think that's pertinent to our discussion."

Brandi stood up, dropped the blanket to the floor and took a couple of steps toward the fireplace. She held her hands out toward the warmth. "I see. I'm supposed to bare my soul to you, but whatever is going on in your life is none of my business." She turned to face him. "That doesn't seem very fair to me." She leveled a stern look in his direction. "How about you? Does that seem fair to you?"

There was no doubt in his mind about the message she had just delivered. He was pushing her too much, too hard and too fast. He needed to back off and let things calm down. He had to keep his own issues off the front burner if he was going to get the information out of her that he wanted.

Reece shifted gears in an attempt to gain her confidence. He extended a warm smile. "I'm hungry. I notice you helped yourself to some soup, but that's not much of a meal. Now that I have food in the refrigerator, could I interest you in some dinner? Maybe a steak and a green salad?"

A tentative smile curled the edges of her lips. "I have to admit that I am hungry. You're right, soup isn't much of a meal and that's the only thing I've had to eat all day."

He went to the kitchen and returned a few minutes later with an opened bottle of wine and two glasses. "My favorite merlot to go with the steak. How do you like yours cooked? Rare, medium…"

"How about a pink center, but not really too red?"

He smiled—a warm, engaging smile. "Consider it done."

Brandi took a sip of her wine as she watched him return to the kitchen. He had a marvelous smile framed by an incredibly handsome face. His eyes were honest, eyes that didn't look away as if they were trying to hide something. And a smooth voice that she suspected could lull anyone into believing whatever he wanted them to believe. Or so it seemed.

She was beginning to relax as the stress started to melt away. For the first time since the nightmare began, she felt a flicker of hope try to assert itself. If Reece Covington truly was a private investigator maybe he could help her. She allowed a slight sigh of resignation. It took more than someone with a handsome face, a hard body and enough sexual magnetism to fill the Grand Canyon to be able to help her. She knew the danger surrounding her would not go away on its own. Should she trust him more than she already had? After all, what did she have to lose?

Only her life, that's all.

She leaned back and closed her eyes. The sound of the rain on the roof mingled with the crackling and popping of the burning wood to form an intimate coziness. With his office in Rocky Shores he certainly would have come into periodic contact with the Rocky Shores police. As a private investigator he surely had occasion to interface with the local police on cases he was working on.

There seemed to be a lot of mystery surrounding him, but she felt somewhat reluctant to question him too much. Her mind drifted to myriad thoughts, some of them about the trouble she was in, some of them about this very disconcerting man and others to what the future held for her. It seemed no time at all before Reece returned with a tray. He set it on the table.

"Dinner is served."

They ate, sipped their wine and engaged in superficial conversation. She immediately recognized his mastery at controlling the situation, including the direction of the conversation and the topics they discussed. If he was even half as good a private investigator as he was at manipulating what went on around him without giving the impression of seeming to be demanding or intimidating, then perhaps he would be the ideal person to help her.

If he really was a private investigator.

And *if* he meant what he said about not harming her.

When they finished eating, he indicated the sofa in

front of the fireplace. He put another log on the fire, then sat down next to her.

"Now that we've had some dinner and you've had an opportunity to relax, perhaps we could get back to the main issue at hand."

She gathered her composure and challenged his take-charge attitude. "Okay, I believe my question was what had happened in your past that you apparently think might be linked to what's going on in my life right now. What kind of a connection are you talking about and why do you think such a connection would even exist?"

He emitted a soft chuckle, amused by her attempt to put him on the defensive. "I meant getting back to your description of what this policeman who abducted you looks like."

"I've answered lots of questions for you. I think it's time you answered at least one of mine."

He turned her words over in his mind. He had to admit that it was a reasonable request. "All right." He chose his words carefully, not wanting to fully disclose the nature of what had happened. "I had a run-in with a Rocky Shores police detective that turned out very bad for me. Ever since then, I've had my suspicions about him, his honesty and his ethics. I'm trying to determine if it could be the same man who abducted you."

"Wouldn't that be a little too coincidental? Something from out of left field?"

"No more so than finding you in my cabin."

Brandi leaned back and slowly nodded her head. "Touché!"

"Besides, we're both connected to Rocky Shores, a

town of only thirty thousand people. I worked there and you live there. That ties it together with some reality rather than mere coincidence, certainly much more than if it had been a large city like Seattle."

He softened his voice to a soothing timbre. "Now, tell me what the man looked like...as much as you can recall."

"Well, I'm five-seven, and he was definitely taller than I am but not as tall as you."

"I'm six foot two. So, would five feet eleven inches be about right? Or would he be a little shorter than that? Or taller?"

"That sounds right...five-eleven. He was average weight for his height. His hair was sort of a sandy brown color with some gray mixed in. I'd say he was in his mid-forties."

The excitement built inside him. His mind raced almost faster than his mouth could keep up with it. "Did you notice the color of his eyes? Any scars, tattoos or other distinguishing marks? A beard or mustache?"

"His eyes? No, I didn't get that good a look at him. As I said, it was only a quick glimpse before he blindfolded me." She wrinkled her brow in concentration. There was something else...something she could almost see, but not quite.

He cocked his head and looked questioningly at her. "Yes?"

"I'm not sure. I know I saw something important, but I can't bring it into focus. It was so fleeting. Maybe I only thought—"

Her body stiffened. A quick jolt of fear crashed

through her when he placed his hand over her eyes. She grabbed his wrist and frantically tried to pull his hand away from her face.

Her sudden burst of fear came out in her voice. "What are you doing?" Had her tentative trust been misplaced? Was this the moment she had dreaded? Was he in league with her stalker? Had she said enough for him to realize that she could be a threat to him?

Reece shoved her hand away. "Just relax. I told you, I'm not going to hurt you. Now, close your eyes and try to visualize what happened. What did he do first? Tell me everything you can remember in the order that it occurred."

Brandi took a calming breath. Had she allowed her fears to shove her imagination into overload? When she wasn't afraid of what he might do, he managed to instill a sense of confidence.

"Okay." She took a calming breath, leaned back and closed her eyes. The scene began to replay through her mind.

"He must have been hiding in my garage, waiting for me. When I opened my car door he came up behind me and put his hand over my mouth. As I struggled to get free he put his other arm across my neck and told me I'd better shut up and behave if I didn't want to get hurt."

"His voice…what did it sound like?"

"I couldn't tell. He whispered the words in my ear, sort of a raspy whisper. I don't know if it was real or if he was attempting to disguise his voice. He shoved me toward the side door of the garage. He turned me loose so he could open the door. That's when I got a glimpse of his face. He put a blindfold over my eyes and steered me out the door and across the backyard toward the alley. I tripped on something, stumbled and fell. My blindfold shifted position. When he reached down to pull me to my feet, I was able to see out from underneath it."

She frowned as she pursed her lips. "That's when I saw his badge…and something else. It was on his arm."

She sat up straight. Her eyes opened wide as if she had just remembered something. "No—it wasn't his arm. It was on his wrist."

Reece's voice grew anxious. "What did you see? A scar? A tattoo? What?"

"I'm not sure. He had something around his wrist. It wasn't a watch. I think it was…" The fuzzy image suddenly popped into focus. She saw it clearly. The excitement filled her voice and surrounded her words. She made eye contact with him. "That's it! It was a medical alert bracelet."

"Were you able to make out what type of medical condition? If he was a policeman, then he would have been in good health so it wouldn't have been something like a heart condition. Perhaps an allergy to some sort of medication?"

"I don't know what it said, but I recognized the medical insignia on it."

A flicker of disappointment rippled through him, dashing his hopes. He quickly shoved it aside and went on to his next question. "The badge…were you able to make out anything beyond the fact that it was a badge? A police department? A federal agency? Anything?"

A dejected Brandi slumped back against the sofa cushions. A definite air of disappointment accompanied her words. "No, just that it was a badge clipped to his belt."

Reece shifted the direction of his questions in an attempt to jog her memory a little more. "Was there anything else on his belt? A holster, perhaps? If he was wearing his badge, then he was probably armed, too. Did you notice anything like that?"

"No, nothing."

"Okay, let's try something else. How was he dressed?"

She furrowed her brow in concentration as she tried to force an image. "He wasn't wearing a suit, but he wasn't dressed in jeans, either. He wore slacks, a shirt that buttoned down the front and tucked in rather than a pullover and some sort of lightweight jacket with a zipper."

"You're doing great, Brandi. Just a little more, now. What color were his clothes?"

"The slacks were a charcoal-gray and the jacket a lighter shade of gray. The shirt was blue."

"That's terrific—good job." He squeezed her hand to show his appreciation.

She looked up at him. His expression showed how pleased he was with what she had been able to recall. A little moment of satisfaction nestled inside her. It was a lot more detail than she realized she had noticed at the time.

There was one more thing she became acutely aware of…Reece's hand still covered hers. Rather than evoking fear, this time his touch filled her with a comfort that she found very reassuring. It was accompanied by a flicker of hope she had not felt since the nightmare began a month ago.

"Does that help at all? Did I remember enough for you to recognize who it was?"

"Well, it wasn't enough for me to be sure about anything, but it will go a long way in identifying who it was if we come across him somewhere along the line."

"*We?*" The excitement bubbled inside her. "Does this mean that you believe me? That you're going to help me?" Maybe there was a way out of this mess after all. She tried to temper her enthusiasm with a more pragmatic approach. "I'll pay for your investigative services, of course. A straightforward business deal."

"We can talk about that later." He withdrew his hand from hers. The moment of intimate contact had infused him with a warmth he had not felt in a long time. The moment he broke the physical contact a sudden feeling of loss flooded through him. That was not a good sign. He needed to double his determination to maintain his emotional distance from this very tempting woman and her obvious vulnerability, which continued to tug at him.

"Do you think you would recognize him if you saw a picture?"

She tilted her head to one side and scrunched up the side of her mouth. "I don't know. I might. As I said, it was only a glimpse." She sat up straight and stared at him. "Do you have pictures of the members of the

Rocky Shores Police Department?" Then she slumped back again. "Of course, he might be a police officer somewhere else, one of the other cities around Seattle or maybe even in Seattle."

A sigh of resignation escaped her throat. "Or maybe he was some sort of security guard and not a law enforcement officer at all."

Reece grabbed another log and put it on the fire. "That's very true. We can't go jumping to conclusions." As much as he wanted to tie together her problem with his, he didn't have anything concrete—only his strong suspicions.

He went to the window, pulled the drape aside and stared out into the darkness. "The rain doesn't seem to be letting up. It looks like it might end up raining all night." And of even more concern to him was what to do about her being in his cabin. Eventually it would be time to go to bed. Should he offer to drive her home? Drive her to a motel?

Suggest that she spend the night in his cabin?

He was never going to keep temptation at arm's length with her sleeping under the same roof with him. A cozy fire, the sound of the rain—a scene ripe for seduction. He sucked in a deep breath, held it for several seconds, then slowly exhaled. What had he gotten himself into? The very notion that her stalking and abduction would have any connection to him being set up and framed for a crime was totally preposterous. He was trying to make two pieces fit together that didn't even belong to the same puzzle.

Reece had been offered parole after only a few

months in prison, but had refused. He had no intention of giving them the opportunity of sending him back to prison with time added on to his sentence by claiming some trumped-up violation of his parole. He did the full term of his sentence and walked out the gates without further obligation to the legal system—no reporting to a parole officer, needing to provide them with his address or having to prove that he had a job.

It had been three months. He had been hiding in his cabin with nothing to do to occupy his time other than read, watch television, surf the Internet and dwell on the past and what had happened to him. Maybe it was time to put that part of his life to rest. To quit thinking about it. To stop fixating on the people who had been responsible.

But that was easier said than done.

He stared at Brandi. She seemed to be lost in thought. Perhaps fate had delivered her into his hands. Even though he no longer had his private investigator's license, he could still put his expertise to use by helping her get to the bottom of the mystery. It would give him a place to focus his energy and help pull him out of his self-pity.

He needed to come up with a plan of action. But first, he had to figure out what they were going to do about sleeping arrangements for that night. He returned to the sofa and sat down next to her.

"Brandi…" He took her hand in his. Once again the physical contact filled him with a warmth that had been missing from his life for far too long. He forced his thoughts to the immediate problem. "We have to figure out what to do about tonight…about sleeping arrangements…about where—"

He felt her muscles tense and her body stiffen.

Chapter Three

Anxiety filled Brandi's voice, and a hint of panic crept into her words. "I can't go home. Whoever it is knows where I live. He might be watching my house at this very minute."

Reece tried to alleviate her sudden surge of panic. "That's what I thought, too. So, we're left with two options. I can drive you to a motel or…uh…" A rush of discomfort told him how awkward he found the situation. "You can spend the night here."

He saw the alarm flash through her eyes and across her face. He rushed his words, afraid she had misinterpreted what he'd said. "This sofa folds out into a bed. I can sleep here and you can have the bedroom."

Brandi stared at him for a moment. She knew she couldn't go home but hadn't really solidified any thoughts about exactly what to do or where to go. She didn't want to jump to conclusions again, assume the worst, but she didn't want him to get the wrong idea either. "I don't want to impose on you like that. I've already abused your hospitality."

With his free hand he gestured toward her dirty

clothes. "You'd probably like something clean to put on and a hot shower, too."

A shy smile slowly formed on her lips. "Yes, that would be nice. But I don't know where I'm going to get any clean clothes tonight."

His words were tentative, escaping into the open before he was sure he wanted to say them. "I could go to your house and bring back what you need."

A quick look of concern flitted across her face. "But if someone is watching my house, they'd see you go inside. You'd be in danger."

He squeezed her hand reassuringly. "Don't you worry about that. I can spot surveillance a mile away, especially if the person watching your house thinks they are dealing with someone who is inexperienced in the method of a stakeout. I know how to get in and out of places without being spotted. So—" he flashed a confident smile "—draw a floor plan of your house, give me your keys and a list of what you want and tell me where to find it. I should be back in a little over two hours. It's normally a one-hour drive to Rocky Shores from here. I should be in and out of your house in less than ten minutes and will come straight back. Of course, it might take a little longer because of the rain on the mountain roads."

"Why can't I go with you? I certainly know where everything is. Wouldn't it be better if I went along?"

"I don't think that's a good idea. If someone is watching your house, I don't want to take a chance on whoever it is seeing you. If they spot you, it could be a dangerous situation. I can take care of myself, but I'd rather not have to take care of both of us. It will be quicker for me to go alone."

"Well...I guess that makes sense." Giving the key to her house to a virtual stranger? It was a decision that left her uneasy, but what did she have to lose at this point? If he truly posed a threat to her, he could have done any number of unpleasant things to her by now.

After all, no one knew where to find her. She was trapped in his cabin—even to the point where he had hauled her back inside when she had tried to run. He had her pinned to the floor and under his complete control.

Yet he had been a man of his word. He had told her he wouldn't hurt her, and he hadn't.

Then another thought occurred to her. Having him gone for a while would give her an opportunity to search the cabin and see if she could find anything other than the very sketchy information he had given her—*reluctantly* given her. Was she merely rationalizing this no-win situation, or was this strategy viable? She wasn't sure.

He may have soothed her shattered nerves a bit, but she was still acutely aware of the very real danger that had chased her to his cabin in the first place and continued to pursue her. She steeled her determination. She needed to take advantage of every opportunity that came her way, and this was no exception.

"Do you have some paper and a pencil so I can draw that floor plan and make you a list?"

He grabbed a notebook and pen from the top of the desk and handed them to her. She sketched the layout of her house, listed a few basic things for him to bring her and where to find them. She tore out the page and handed it to him along with her keys.

"Here, this should do it."

He took the paper from her, started to leave, then paused. He turned to face her, his voice soft and conveying his genuine concern. "Lock the door behind me. Don't open it for anyone, no matter who they say they are. I'll use my key to get in when I return."

Her words were filled with emotion. "Please…be careful."

He extended a confident smile, then the smile faded. It was as if he didn't have any conscious control over his own actions. He brushed his fingertips across her cheek, cupped her chin in his hand and leaned his face into hers. He placed a soft kiss on her lips. His words held the same emotion as hers had. "Don't worry. I'm always careful." He allowed his hand to linger for a moment before breaking the enticing physical contact.

Brandi watched as he pulled on a rain jacket and stepped out onto the front porch. He brought the hood over his head, then made a dash for his car. She shut and locked the front door and listened as he started the engine and drove away.

She suddenly felt very much alone. It had only been a few hours since Reece had found her in his cabin. During that time, she had been fearful of the danger he represented, petrified when he'd chased her out into the storm and forcibly brought her back to the cabin, then terrified out of her wits when he'd tackled her and pinned her to the floor. But he had let her up as he'd promised and had done his best to make her comfortable. She had to admit that he had managed to ease her fears and worries and even instill a modicum of confidence. He seemed a man of his word.

She touched her fingers to her lips. The heat of the brief kiss continued to linger there. She didn't know what to think. Was she being played for a fool? Was this all part of some master plan he had devised? She shook her head. If he was somehow involved, why would he have gone off and left her alone to escape? True, he had her house keys, but not having a key certainly wouldn't stop someone from entering her house.

She attempted to dismiss the conflicting thoughts and her emotional upheaval by turning her attention to other matters.

The desk against the far wall—there would probably be something in the desk that would tell her more about him. If nothing else, at least something that could confirm his name.

She swallowed down the nervousness churning in the pit of her stomach as she slowly crossed the room to the desk. She reached out a trembling hand, then paused. The same feeling of guilt washed through her as it had when she'd crawled in his kitchen window. What she was doing was wrong. But she also told herself that the present circumstances were anything but normal.

Her confusion ran rampant, leaving her emotions in turmoil. He had been right. She wanted to believe him. To believe that he was an honorable man. To believe that he could and would help her.

To believe that she could trust him.

She pulled open the drawer and withdrew several file folders, placing them on top of the desk. Then she opened a large bottom drawer where she found a laptop computer resting on top of several large envelopes.

REECE DROVE DOWN Brandi's street, taking careful note of every parked car. He didn't drive so slowly that he would look suspicious to the neighbors, but slowly enough that he didn't miss anything. Her sketch indicated a gate from the back alley to her yard and a side door from the yard to the garage. He could enter the house that way without anyone in front seeing him. But first, he wanted to make sure no one was watching from the street.

For an hour he had turned things over in his mind as he drove from his cabin to her house. Had he just been pulled into another bad situation by a beautiful woman who appeared vulnerable and seemed in need of his help? Was he being set up again, only this time with a longer prison sentence waiting on the horizon? But could he afford to pass up an opportunity to even things with Frank James, no matter what the risk? He wasn't at all sure he was doing the right thing.

Had he ended up frightening Brandi more than instilling a sense of confidence? He touched his fingers to the scratches on the side of his face. Yes, indeed—she had fought to protect herself. Unfortunately, he had been on the receiving end of her attack. After that, had he managed to assuage her fears?

Suddenly, a flicker of light caught his attention, snapping his mind away from his thoughts and back to the task at hand. The breath froze in his lungs. His senses went on full alert. A man was sitting in a car parked across the street from Brandi's house, his cigarette lighter supplying just enough illumination to see the man's face. There was no doubt in his mind—Detective Sergeant Frank James, recently promoted to the rank of lieutenant.

Years of anger and resentment twisted in his gut, turning his insides into a seething cauldron. It took all his conscious control to continue driving in a straight line at the same speed and not do anything to arouse suspicion. When he arrived at the corner he made a left turn so that he could come back through the alley behind Brandi's house. As soon as he was out of the lieutenant's line of sight, he pulled over to the curb and stopped.

His worst nightmare and his foremost obsession all rolled up into one. Frank James—the crooked cop who had lied on the witness stand. The man responsible for sending him to prison. Frank James and his cohort, an enticing and devious little sexpot named Cindy Thatcher. Cindy had played him for a fool from day one, and he had been so dazzled that he hadn't seen it coming.

Reece had a turbulent ten-year history with Frank. It had started when Frank had arrested a murder suspect, insisting that the man was guilty beyond any doubt—almost as if it had been a personal matter for him. The suspect's attorney had hired Reece to find evidence to verify his client's alibi. Reece had been able to do it, and the man had been acquitted. Reece later found out that the man's arrest had, indeed, been a personal matter on the part of Frank James.

After that, it had seemed that every time Reece had turned around, a case he was involved with ended up having something to do with Frank James. Twice Frank had attempted to get his private investigator's license revoked on the flimsiest of excuses, and twice he had failed.

What in the world could Brandi be involved in that had put a piece of vindictive scum like Frank James on her trail?

He clenched his jaw in determination and tried to tamp down his bitter resentment. If she had somehow crossed this rogue cop, then it was as much his fight as it was hers. She was ill-equipped to handle a confrontation with Frank on her own. If nothing else, that settled the matter in his mind. Frank James was his prey—and nothing would stand in his way in bringing Frank down.

True, Brandi's sketchy description of her abductor could fit any number of men, but Frank James was definitely one of them. A little flicker of satisfaction told him things were about to break wide open, that inner voice and instinct he had learned to trust over the years, especially during his time in prison. If only he had trusted that voice earlier, back when it had tried to tell him Cindy Thatcher was bad news.

Suddenly the world had come alive with a promise of a future. He had found a purpose, a way to focus his energy and revitalize his existence. And that purpose was to expose Frank James and bring down his network.

Reece drove down the alley behind Brandi's house with his headlights turned off. He stopped two houses from her back fence, turned off the engine and sat for a few minutes going over everything in his mind. The reason he had given Brandi for her staying behind had been the truth—as far as it went. But he had another reason for not wanting her to go with him. He wanted to do more than just pick up the things on her list. He also wanted to look around inside her house, to get a better feel for who she was and see if he could find anything that might give him a clue to what was happening and why. But with Frank James sitting out in front, he needed to be careful.

Very careful.

Frank James epitomized obnoxious, unethical, dishonest and arrogant. He represented a slap in the face to all the law enforcement officers who worked hard to keep the public safe while placing their own lives in daily jeopardy. But there was one thing Frank James was not—he was not a fool.

Reece didn't want to enter Brandi's house while Frank was still parked in front. He made his way across her backyard and stationed himself in the bushes where he could see Frank's car.

And then he waited.

Stakeouts weren't new to him, but it had been a long time since he had experienced the excitement of being on a case. The adrenaline surge told him he was back where he belonged. Even the steady rainfall didn't dampen his enthusiasm. And he had the added benefit of knowing it was more than just being on a case again. His one burning obsession, clearing his name while bringing down the man responsible for putting him in prison, had just taken on a new life. It had moved into the realm of reality.

Less than half an hour later Frank started his car and pulled away from the curb. Reece waited another fifteen minutes to make sure Frank wasn't circling the neighborhood in an effort to make it appear that he had gone.

He pulled Brandi's keys from his pocket and entered the garage from the side door. Once safely out of sight, he shrugged out of his rain jacket and shook off the water. He took off his boots and left them in the garage so he wouldn't track mud inside her house. He pulled the flashlight from his pocket.

Using her sketch, he slowly made his way through the interior, room by room. Everything in the living room, dining room and kitchen seemed to be normal, or at least what he assumed to be normal. Everything was neat, clean and orderly. Nothing appeared to have been disturbed. He looked around her bedroom and bathroom. Things there seemed to be in place, too. He collected the items she had on her list, placing them in a small suitcase from her closet.

Then he checked her office, a storage room, her darkroom and what would have been another bedroom that she was using as a studio. In sharp contrast to the rest of her house, it seemed obvious that someone had searched these rooms. While her picture files had not been vandalized, someone had definitely been looking for something specific. He had no way of knowing what they had been searching for or if anything was missing.

What could someone have been looking for? Or more accurately, what could Frank James be looking for? Why would pictures of weddings and portrait sittings be of interest to him? What could they have to do with the nightmare that had invaded her life? Even the photographs for the book she said she was working on, scenic pictures from around the state, didn't seem to be anything that would pose a threat to anyone.

If Brandi had purposely hidden something in her picture files, then she would know what someone had been after and why she had become a target. But he believed her story. He believed she was very frightened and didn't know why any of this was happening to her.

Two televisions, a VCR and a DVD player, a computer, camera equipment and darkroom equipment—items easily turned into cash—had not been disturbed. He returned to her bedroom and checked the jewelry box. Unless there was a particular piece of jewelry missing, everything appeared to be undisturbed.

So, the disarray in her office was not the work of a common burglar. Had whoever it was found what he had been looking for? It was a question he couldn't answer. Would Brandi be able to?

Reece pulled a small digital camera from his pocket and thoroughly documented the condition of her work areas. Maybe the pictures would trigger something for her that could help them figure out what was going on. As an afterthought, he also took pictures of the other rooms in case there was something missing that was not obvious to him. He worked quickly, dimming the flash so it wouldn't be visible to curious eyes outside.

He glanced at his watch. He had stayed there longer than he had intended to on top of the long wait before he could enter the house. He would be very late getting back to the cabin, and he had no way of contacting her to let her know what was happening.

He made one last survey of her office and darkroom. A strange thought began to form in the back of his mind, something so obscure that it seemed almost ridiculous. But not so ridiculous that he could completely dismiss it. A thought about why someone had rummaged through her picture files.

Before leaving, he grabbed the business appointment book from her desktop, the PDA from the drawer, then turned on her computer and checked her security software to make sure he could access her hard drive from his laptop computer.

He returned to the cabin as quickly as the road conditions allowed. Would she still be there, or would she have taken advantage of his absence and left his cabin? Surely she wouldn't be so foolish as to wander around in the woods on foot in a rainstorm at night. Or would she? Would his impulsive kiss have frightened her, made her afraid of what might happen if she stayed in his cabin overnight? Was she still wary about him having been physical with her to get her back inside the cabin? She should know that if he were the type of man who would attack her he would already have done it, but that didn't mean she was thinking with her logic rather than her emotions. He again touched his fingers to the scratches on his cheek.

Stupid...stupid...stupid. Why did I kiss her? Why couldn't I have left the cabin as I'd planned, without indulging the temptation?

By the time he pulled off the fire road and parked in his carport, over three and a half hours had passed, much longer than he had told her. He was tired, but the excitement of being involved in a case again had kept his adrenaline pumping.

And the chance to get at Frank James had made his spirits soar.

Reece unlocked the door and stepped inside. The cabin was quiet and the room empty. His muscles tensed and an adrenaline surge put his senses on high alert. He called to her, forcing a casualness to his voice that did not exist. "Brandi…it's me. I'm a little late, but I'm back."

He maintained his position by the front door as his gaze raked the room, searching for anything that was out of place. He spotted the papers on the dining table—his release papers from prison. A quick jolt of panic hit him. He hadn't been prepared for this. He called her name again.

"Brandi…"

A moment later she emerged from the bathroom. Her strained voice told him she had forced a calm to her words. "I was starting to worry. I thought you might have had problems because of the rain and the mountain roads…or something."

He saw the wariness in her eyes and the way she seemed to be using the furniture as a barrier between them. He knew he could not sidestep this one by telling her it was none of her business. He had forcibly carried her back inside the cabin when she'd tried to leave. That sort of made it her business. She had the right to know who he was...within reason. But exactly how much should he tell her? He also knew it would be better if he brought up the subject rather than waiting for her to do it. That way, he could control the direction of the conversation.

He gestured toward the papers on the table. As the old adage said, the best defense was a good offense. He carefully chose his words in an attempt to throw her off balance and keep control.

"I see you've been snooping in my desk and going through my personal papers."

Her eyes widened in surprise at his accusation. She nervously shifted her weight from one foot to the other. She didn't like what he'd said, but she couldn't deny it. "Well, uh...no, I...well, I did happen to see—"

He picked up the papers from the table top and glanced through them. "Yes, I can see what you *happened* to come across in your *innocent* perusal of my belongings—something that was inside an envelope under my laptop computer in the bottom drawer of my desk. They were practically on public display, just waiting for someone to come along and see them."

He turned his back on her as he took off his rain jacket and hung it on the coat hook by the door. Then he pulled off his muddy boots. He turned and faced her again.

"And now I suppose you'd like to have an explanation?"

"Well, I was sort of wondering..." Her voice trailed off. She didn't know what to say or how to respond to his attack. What in the world had possessed her to leave the papers on the table rather than putting them back where she had found them? Her initial thought had seemed like a good idea at the time. She had intended to use it as a means of forcing him to tell her about himself—an exchange of information for what he had managed to wheedle out of her. She had hoped seeing the papers on the table would throw him off guard, leave him unnerved and a little rattled so she could have the upper hand. But whatever the reason, it now seemed very foolish.

She looked up at him. His face held an impassive expression. His eyes weren't angry, but they were intense. A new wave of anxiety washed through her body, one that put her on edge. She tried to analyze the situation. Was she in trouble? Had she stepped over some invisible line from safety into danger? Was this the proverbial straw that broke the camel's back? She swallowed in an attempt to lessen the lump in her throat.

Reece fixed her with a steady gaze. "I was released from prison three months ago, after serving the full two-year term of my sentence. I'm not on parole. My arrest and subsequent conviction was a travesty of justice. I did not do what I was convicted of. I was set up and framed."

She glanced down at the floor. "Of course." That really wasn't an explanation. Didn't everyone in prison claim to be innocent? At least that's the way it seemed. She regained eye contact with him. "Exactly what were you convicted of doing?"

A snort of disgust escaped his throat. "What was I convicted of? I guess you could say I was convicted of trying to help a lady in distress who had retained my services as a private investigator."

She swallowed the apprehension trying to work its way up her throat. "What does that mean?"

"It means I was not convicted of a violent crime or anything having to do with drugs, if that's your concern. You're not in danger from me." He folded his arms across his chest and stared at her. "All I can do is tell you that what I'm saying is the truth. Whether you choose to believe me or not is up to you. Now, do you want to dwell on this, or do you want to know what I found at your house?" He picked up the small suitcase he had placed on the floor and held it out toward her. "Other than the items on your list."

She took a couple of tentative steps forward and accepted the suitcase from him. "Thank you." Now what? He admitted to having been in prison yet made no attempt to explain what had happened beyond saying he was innocent. And two years wasn't a very long sentence. She knew that much was true because she had seen the dates on the papers. It wasn't like having been convicted of murder or armed robbery or some other sort of violent crime.

She clenched her jaw. She was rationalizing again. He had made it very clear that he had no intention of discussing it any further. Should she push him for more information or let it drop? An uneasiness welled inside her. She knew her position was tenuous. As he had said, he was bigger and stronger than her. He had physical control of the situation. So, she had to concentrate on being more clever—at least until she had her concerns about him settled in her mind. But for now there were more immediate matters to consider.

His comment about finding something at her house had grabbed her attention and continued to circulate through her mind. Perhaps that would be a more prudent path to follow for right now. But she had to admit that she couldn't shake the notion that there was an indefinable quality about him that went deeper than what he had shown on the outside. It said he was an honorable man despite having been in prison.

She knew exactly how vulnerable she was. She had given it a lot of thought while he was gone. Isolated in a mountain cabin with a man she had never seen before. A man who had just been released from prison. A man who could have taken advantage of her if he'd wanted to. And she had not objected when he'd kissed her—only a brief kiss, not much more than a brushing of the lips, but still a kiss. He could certainly have taken that as encouragement. There was no way she could have physically stopped him. But, she hadn't needed to. His behavior had been above board.

Could she really trust this stranger who had served time in prison? She tried to regain her composure. Did she have any other options at the moment? She would take it one step at a time.

"You said you found something at my house?" She looked at him questioningly. "What did you find?"

He didn't answer her. Instead, he took the digital camera from his pocket and removed the card. Next, he took the laptop computer from the desk, plugged it in and turned it on.

Curiosity got the best of her. She edged her way over to the desk to see what he was up to. "What are you doing? Why won't you answer my question about what you found?"

"I'm about to show you. I took lots of pictures. Give me a few minutes and I'll have them downloaded into the computer, then you can see them large size on the screen." As the photographs were transferred from the card to the computer hard drive, he took her appointment book and PDA from his jacket and set them on the desk.

Before he brought the pictures up on the screen, he edged into the conversation he really wanted. "Tell me, do you know someone named Frank James?"

A little frown wrinkled across her forehead. "Frank James? The only Frank James I know of is the outlaw—the one who was Jesse James's brother."

"No, not that Frank James—" a bittersweet chuckle escaped his throat "—although there's more similarity than one would suspect." He turned to face her. "The Frank James I'm referring to is a detective lieutenant with the Rocky Shores Police Department. Do you know him? Could you have met him when you tried to report your stalker?"

Brandi slowly shook her head as she turned the name over in her mind. "No…it doesn't ring any bells. Is there some reason why I should know him?"

"I just thought you might." He paused a moment, wanting to observe her reaction to what he was about to say. "He was watching your house tonight. He didn't see me, but I sure saw him. He was staked out across the street in his car."

Her eyes widened in shock. A cold tremor rippled through her body followed by a wave of apprehension. Had she heard him correctly? "A police detective was watching my house? Are you sure?"

"Yes, I'm sure." Her surprise seemed genuine to him.

"And you think it was this Frank James you mentioned?"

"I *know* it was." He turned back to his computer. "That's one of the reasons I was late. I had to wait half an hour before I went inside. I didn't want to enter your house while he was still there, even though he wouldn't have been able to see me. It wouldn't have been wise for me to take a chance on him entering your house while I was in there."

She tried to temper the sudden wave of apprehension that swept through her body with some logic. "Perhaps the police decided to take my stalking report seriously. Maybe he was assigned to watch my house…as some sort of protection for me?"

"I sincerely doubt it."

Brandi sank into the corner of the sofa. She felt as if all the life had been kicked out of her and there was no fight left. She had been battling with her unknown stalker for so long that she didn't know what to do or think anymore. A police detective watching her house. A policeman abducting her. She tried to calm her rattled nerves. Her gaze became riveted to the floor, and she was unable to meet Reece's pointed stare.

"This detective watching my house…Frank James…" She looked up, making tentative eye contact with him. His eyes were so intense. Whatever was going on inside him was something he felt very deeply. "Do you think he could be the policeman who abducted me? I know it was a very general description, but does he look like he could be the person I described?"

He held her eye contact without answering her question. He again wondered just how much information he should share with her. How much of his personal pain he should let out into the open. Once again her vulnerability pulled at his senses. And once again he felt himself being drawn further and further inside her turmoil—a place he didn't want to be. A place that could interfere with his need to even the score with Frank James.

He tempered his words with caution. He didn't want to give her the impression that her nightmare was all but over simply because he had identified Frank James.

"Yes, your description does fit him. But it could fit lots of other people, too."

"WHAT THE HELL DID YOU THINK you were doing, Frank? You just took it upon yourself to grab her?" The fifty-year-old man shook his head in disgust, then leveled a stern look at his cohort. "What did you think you were going to accomplish with that stupid bit of business?"

Frank's angry words showed his resentment at being summoned in the middle of the night and treated like an underling, but he was not angry enough to become engaged in a physical confrontation with someone who could have him blown away with one phone call. "Your way wasn't working. We weren't getting anywhere with her. I went through her files and took everything even remotely relevant."

"Brilliant! So then you grabbed her and compounded that stupidity by letting her get away. And now she knows that she's actually in physical danger. She'll discover what you took, and she might even be able to put two and two together. All she has to do is stroll into the Rocky Shores police station and see you there. That will certainly blow everything wide open."

Frank leaned forward, his hands on the desk as he confronted his business partner with an intimidating stare. "I blindfolded her. And even if she did get a quick glimpse of me it will be her word against mine. She has no proof of anything. When she tried to report her *stalker,* the desk sergeant almost laughed her out of the station because her story was so preposterous."

"You'd better be right, Frank." There was no mistaking the thinly veiled threat contained in his voice.

"You should have let me take care of her from the beginning just like I wanted to."

"You know that would have been a stupid move. We have to know if there are any other copies anywhere and whether she's told anyone. Until we know, we need to proceed carefully. Our *friends* aren't going to be pleased."

"I could have done it without them knowing."

He stared pointedly at Frank James. "You already screwed up when you grabbed her, then you screwed up a second time when you let her get away. One more screwup like that and I'm sure they will graphically demonstrate just how displeased they are. Three strikes can be fatal."

He rose to his feet and came out from behind the

mahogany desk. Even though he was an inch or two shorter than Frank, his presence dominated the room. He leveled one final hard look at Frank, then walked down the hallway to his living room, opened the front door and stood aside. Frank had clearly and decisively been dismissed.

He watched as Frank got into his car and drove away. Then he poured himself a scotch as he vented what had been his carefully controlled anger. The words were mumbled out loud even though there was no one to hear them.

"Frank has been an invaluable aide in the past, but he's handled this little mess like some stupid amateur. Perhaps he's outlived his usefulness."

He took a deep drink from his glass, then set it down and reached for the phone. "Our *friends* aren't going to like this…not one bit."

Chapter Four

For the next two hours Reece and Brandi went through all the pictures he had taken at her house. He added his impressions of what he had found as it related to each picture. She confirmed that the pictures he took didn't reveal anything missing, but her photograph files in the office were another story. However, just because someone had gone through them didn't automatically mean something was missing.

She glanced at him. "I'll need to go through those files personally to determine if anything was taken."

"You know as well as I do that it's not a good idea for you to go to your house, especially now that we know it's being watched." A frown wrinkled across his forehead for a moment as he turned a thought over in his mind. "I can bring your files here. That way you will have enough time to give them a thorough search, and you can do it in the light rather than by flashlight."

She shook her head as she spoke. "That won't work. I wouldn't even know what to tell you to bring. Besides, you can't pick up all my file cabinets by yourself and carry them to your car, even if they would fit inside."

A sigh of exasperation escaped his throat. "Yeah, I suppose that's right."

"I can't imagine what there would be in my files that would be of interest to anyone or of any value. There's nothing but negatives and prints, and none of it is anything secret or classified. I have photos of the same scenery that anyone could take a picture of, and as far as the photographs of people are concerned...well, wedding pictures and posed portraits are hardly classified top secret, and none of my clients were celebrities."

Reece glanced at his watch, then reached over and shut down the computer. "I don't know what else we can do tonight."

He turned in his chair to face her. For the last fifteen minutes his mind had barely clung to what they were doing. Most of his attention had been on what the rest of the night would hold—an unsettling topic at best.

He gestured toward the suitcase he had brought her. "Now that you have some clean clothes, I assume you'd like that hot shower."

"Yes, most definitely." She rose from her chair and picked up the suitcase. She opened it and looked at what he had brought. Everything she had asked for was there plus an additional couple of days' worth of clean clothes. Was that indicative of his plans or merely a precaution on his part?

He noted the frown that crossed her face, then it turned to a look of uncertainty. "What's wrong? Did I forget something?"

"No, it's not that. I was just thinking that, well...maybe before I take a shower and change clothes..."

"What?" A little tremor of apprehension tugged at him. She obviously had something on her mind.

She looked up, making eye contact with him. "I think we should go back to my house so I can look through my picture files."

It was the last thing he had expected her to say. "Are you sure you want to do it tonight?" He glanced at his watch. "It's after eleven o'clock, and it's an hour drive to your house. Obviously we can't do it during the day, but we can do it tomorrow night."

"No, I think we should do it now." She tried to shove aside the anxiety churning in the pit of her stomach. "If Frank James was watching my house earlier this evening, there's no telling what he might do tomorrow night. I need to check my files now before he decides to break in to my house and steal them. If I can figure out which files someone had been looking through, then maybe we can figure out what's going on." She forced what she hoped was a confident smile even though it was a far stretch from what she felt. "And you know I'm the only one who can figure out what, if anything, is missing."

"Yes, I know." He couldn't stop the slight frown that wrinkled across his forehead. He could tell by looking that she was attempting to put up a brave front. He could also see the determination etched into her features. It was the type of expression that stated loud and clear that there wasn't any use in trying to change her mind. And she had been right, it's what they needed to do. They had to stay one step ahead of Frank James if they were going to solve the puzzle. A tremor of apprehension jittered inside him when he realized he had turned his thoughts to them doing it together rather than him doing it alone.

She put her feet back into her damp, muddy shoes. “So, let’s get started. If I’m going to be out in the rain again, then I’ll save the shower and clean clothes until we get back.”

“Okay. Another trip into the rain.” Her comment about returning to the cabin rather than going to a motel was not lost on him. He pulled on his boots, grabbed his rain jacket and handed one to her.

Reece opened the door and stepped out onto the porch. “Are you ready to make a dash to the car?”

A couple of minutes later they pulled out onto the fire road and were soon headed for Rocky Shores. He saw the anxiety etched on her face. He made a couple of attempts at casual conversation, but her abbreviated responses made it clear that she didn’t want to talk. He respected her wishes and remained silent for the rest of the trip, allowing his thoughts to wander to his trial, the lies Frank James had told on the witness stand and his subsequent two years in prison. If nothing else, it reinforced his determination to get the proof he needed to bring Frank down. And apparently Brandi was the key that would open that door for him.

By the time they reached their destination, the rain had been reduced to a drizzle. Reece drove by her house, checking out the few cars parked at the curb. The same excited surge of adrenaline that had assaulted his senses earlier that evening had put him back in the middle of the work he loved to do. Rather than parking in the alley behind her house as he had earlier that evening, he chose to park on the next street, where his car would not be obvious to anyone checking out the alley. They made their way back to her house, crossed the backyard and entered the garage through the side door.

Before going to her office, Brandi made a quick tour of the rest of the house. "Nothing seems to be missing, at least not anything obvious. My televisions, VCR and DVD player are all here." She checked her jewelry box. "Nothing missing from here, either. Let's check my files."

She came to an abrupt halt at the door of her office. The room hadn't been ransacked, but it was obvious that someone had gone through everything. She had seen the pictures, but was still unprepared for the actual sight. She turned and shot a questioning look at Reece.

"Nope, not me. This is exactly the way I found it. Other than taking your appointment book, your PDA and turning on your computer, I didn't touch anything in your office, supply room, darkroom or studio. Your office was a mess compared to the rest of your house, so I assumed someone must have gone through your files. Since there was no way for me to know what you had in here, there was no point in my disturbing anything while trying to figure it out."

A sigh of resignation escaped her lips. "Well, it's not like they ransacked my office, tore up my files and threw everything all over the place, but they definitely went through my files and left them a mess." She went to her darkroom and looked inside, then to her studio and finally to the supply room. Someone had looked through everything. She returned to the office and started going through her picture files.

"Is there anything I can do to help you?"

"No. It's quicker to do it myself than to try and tell someone else what to do."

Reece watched as she checked everything. The way she moved excited him. There was something about her that had grabbed on to him and had refused to let go in spite of how much he didn't want it to be so. But it did not prevent him from noticing the concern that marred her otherwise beautiful features. Even though she tried, she couldn't hide the apprehension that showed in the depth of her eyes. And it tugged at his senses in a very personal way that he wished he could ignore. It frightened him, emotionally if nothing else.

Her voice broke into his errant thoughts, an interruption he welcomed.

"I only did a quick search, but so far the only things missing are the negatives and prints of some of the location photography I did for the book I'm working on."

"When did you take them?"

"I've been doing location shooting for my book off and on for almost a year. I don't know if it turns out to be lucky or unlucky, but the pictures weren't all filed in the same place. I shot the most recent series of photographs during the last month. A month ago is when I started a new file and that's what seems to be missing."

"A month ago?" He scrunched up his face and stared at the floor as he turned the information over in his mind. He regained eye contact with her. "About the time the stalking started?"

She wrinkled her brow into a slight frown. "Yes, it was about that time." She stared at him for a moment. "Do you think there's a connection?"

"What were you photographing? What was on the film?"

"It was just some scenery—beauty shots. I'm putting together scenic photos for what I hope will be one of those expensive coffee-table books filled with beautiful pictures. It's going to take me a year to do all the photography because I want to capture all the seasons. It's a departure for me from weddings and portraits, but I've really been enjoying the challenge. I can't imagine why anyone would want to take those pictures. They don't have any monetary value."

"They obviously had some kind of value to someone and the fact that they only took the ones from the last month rather than all of them says those specific pictures were their target."

"I suppose they could have missed the other scenic shots since they weren't with the ones stolen."

"Are they labeled the same way as the missing pictures? I mean, the file folders showing the same type of information so that it would be obvious to anyone that they were part of the same project? That the pictures they didn't take are part of the same thing as the ones they took?"

"Yes, only the dates would have been different—"

The sound cut into their conversation, grabbing both Reece's and Brandi's attention. A car—it didn't drive by. It had stopped. He immediately clicked off the flashlight, then peeked out the window from the edge of the drapes. A quick rush jumped his pulse rate into high gear as he watched Frank James emerge from the car.

Reece grabbed Brandi's arm and pulled her over to the window. "Look carefully. Is that the man who abducted you?"

The insistence that surrounded his words sent a quick jab of trepidation shooting up her spine. She squinted as she tried to make out the man's features in the illumination from the street light. "I…I'm not sure. It looks like it could be, but I wouldn't be able to swear to it in court without a better look at him." She turned toward Reece. The serious set of his clenched jaw told her more than she wanted to know. "Is that Frank James?"

His words were rushed, telling her of the urgency. "Yes, and it looks like he's coming inside. We've got to get the hell out of here right now!"

There was no time to think, only time to act. They raced through the house, Brandi taking the lead in the dark as they made their way through her familiar surroundings. Just as they exited the garage into the yard, he heard Frank yell to someone else to check the back of the house and the alley.

A cold shiver swept through his body. Frank was not alone. Reece grabbed Brandi's hand. "Whatever I tell you to do, act immediately and don't pause to ask me any questions." Without waiting for any acknowledgment from her, he broke into a run across the backyard. His senses remained on full alert. The blood pumped and his heart pounded. A strange combination of elevated thrill tempered with caution swept through his consciousness. Suddenly, the last two years faded into the far recesses of his mind. He was back in the thick of the action again. For the first time in a long while he felt truly alive. He hadn't realized just how much he had missed it until that moment.

And the icing on the cake was the opportunity to match wits with Frank James again. This time, he would put the crooked cop away while clearing his own record and having his private investigator's license reinstated.

A quick glance at Brandi reminded him that there was more at stake than his own safety and his personal agenda. For some unknown reason she was Frank's target and he knew just how ruthless Frank could be. They reached the alley behind her house. He heard the sound of a car, then he saw it turn from the street into the alley with its headlights off. He pulled her down behind some bushes.

His words came out in a rushed whisper. "Are all the yards along here fenced in or is there a yard open between this alley and the next street over where we parked?"

"The Gleasons, three houses down on the left. Their yard is open all the way through."

"As soon as the car passes that's where we're going. Stay low as you cross the alley." He heard her rapid breathing and could almost feel the tension coursing through her body. Judging by the tight grip she had on his hand, she was anything but calm. And he couldn't blame her. The cat-and-mouse game they had become involved in was no place for a novice.

Reece watched as the car moved slowly down the alley. As soon as it reached the street he gave a little squeeze to her hand. "Let's go."

Brandi sucked in a deep breath in an attempt to calm her trembling insides. She continued to hold on to his hand, to draw from his strength, as they ran down the alley to the open yard. They emerged on the next street two houses down from where they had parked. She started to breathe a little easier, but it was a short-lived moment of calm.

As soon as they were inside his car, Reece grabbed her arm. "Get down!"

The command that surrounded his words clearly reinforced his earlier instruction to *act now and ask questions later.* The fear surged through her body. Her mouth went dry and her throat tried to close. Her heart pounded in her chest. Were they about to be caught? What had he seen? Or had he heard something? She strained to listen, then she heard it. The sound of a car coming closer. She huddled down in the seat. A moment later his body covered hers like a protective cloak, a sensation that helped quell the fear rapidly welling inside her.

It also conveyed a totally inappropriate wave of sensual heat and desire, one she didn't know how to relate to.

He spoke in whispered tones. "A car without headlights, probably the same one that drove down the alley. It could be Frank's cohort checking the area. Or it could be Frank, himself."

She forced her words, fully aware of the anxiety that filled her voice. "Do you think they're looking for us?"

"Probably not us specifically. My guess is that they're checking the area in general just as a precaution." He said the words but knew they weren't true. There was no doubt in his mind that Frank suspected someone had been inside her house. Even though Reece had been careful not to point the flashlight at the windows or wave the light-beam around, it was still possible that Frank might have seen the light as he drove by, which had prompted him to stop. Perhaps it was nothing more than Frank's hunch. Either way, they were in a precarious situation and he needed to be very careful about how he handled it. He had full confidence in his ability to take care of himself even though he didn't have any type of weapon with him, but there was more at stake. Brandi's safety was in his hands, too.

He listened as the car came closer, then moved away as it passed them and continued down the street. He cautiously raised his head enough to see out the window, the streetlights being both a curse and a blessing. He could see, but that meant he could also be seen. As soon as he was satisfied that everything was clear, he sat up and started his car. He slowly pulled away from the curb, not wanting to appear obvious. He drove in the opposite direction than the other car had traveled.

Brandi finally raised herself up enough to peer over the dashboard. Her tentative voice and hesitant words clearly conveyed the wariness and anxiety coursing through her body. "Is…is everything okay? Have they gone?"

"We'll soon know." He knew it wasn't the answer she wanted, but it was the best he could do. He waited until he turned the corner at the end of the block and was headed toward the highway before clicking on his headlights. His gaze constantly darted between the road in front of him, the side streets he passed and his rearview and side mirrors. A low level hum of apprehension remained constant in his body, reminding him that they were a long way from being in the clear. He glanced at Brandi. Her anxiety-ridden features and vulnerability tugged at his emotions—again.

Somehow, Reece was exactly where he had been three years ago when he'd first encountered Cindy Thatcher—trying to help a woman in distress, protect her from harm and finding himself in a dangerous situation because of it. Only with Cindy, she had sought him out and engaged his services as a private investigator. She had told him her brother was missing and she feared he was in danger. It had turned out to be a complete lie and he had ended up serving a two-year prison term for something he didn't do.

And here he was starting down the same path again—a beautiful woman who appeared vulnerable and in need of help. Was history repeating itself?

He cleared the disturbing thoughts from his mind. He needed to keep his attention focused on the current problem, not dwell on something from the past that couldn't be changed. And the current problem was Frank James. He reached over and placed his hand on top of hers, the gesture telling her everything would work out okay.

Reece's touch sent a warm sensation through her body. His strong command and confidence kept her from caving in when everything seemed blackest. She finally had someone who believed her. And more than that, he had put himself in danger in order to help her. She had felt so alone and been so frightened for the past month, since the stalking had begun. Maybe things would turn out okay after all, and she could—

Reece suddenly jammed down his foot on the accelerator. The car lurched forward, shaking Brandi out of her random thoughts. A surge of fear shot her senses to full alert. "What's wrong?"

"We're being followed."

She tried to keep her voice calm. "Will they be able to trace your license plate so they'll know who you are and where you live?"

"Not without a lot of digging and time. My cabin and vehicle ownership are hidden behind a series of—"

He stopped mid-sentence as he executed a perfect 180-degree spin so that he raced toward his pursuer. He clenched his jaw into a hard line. He knew his decision was a calculated risk but one that paid off when the other car swerved out of the way as Reece sped by. He made a sharp right-hand turn at the corner, then another right-hand turn into the grocery store parking lot. He came out on a side street. He knew every back alley and side street in Rocky Shores. Of course, Frank James was a member of the Rocky Shores Police Department and also knew the city streets. It would take more than just a couple of clever maneuvers if it was Frank who was driving the car following them.

But he knew just where to lose even the bulldog determination of Frank James. No one knew the mountain back roads as well as Reece Covington, something his pursuer was about to find out. The adrenaline pumped hard and fast, sending the excitement surging through his body, tempered with a cautionary dose of anxiety.

"Have we lost whoever it was? What do we do now?"

He heard the apprehension in her voice and knew he had to say something to reassure her, to try to calm her obviously rattled nerves. He reached over and placed his hand on top of hers again. He felt the tension rippling just under the surface of her skin. She was trying to appear calm and in control, but it didn't fool him for a minute. He knew she was scared.

And rightly so.

"Try not to worry. I know that's easier to say than it is to do, but everything is going to be all right." He flashed a confident smile. "I promise." He wasn't sure exactly how he was going to keep that promise, but somehow he had to make it happen.

Reece headed out of town toward the Cascade Mountains. He spotted his pursuer, but now the car was staying back and tailing him rather than trying to catch him. A self-satisfied grin tugged at the corners of his mouth. Whoever was driving had just made a major mistake. The sedan was no match on the muddy back roads for his four-wheel drive SUV. He took a sharp turn onto a narrow, winding mountain road.

Brandi took a deep breath and held it for several seconds. Her heart jumped into her throat and her pulse raced. She looked out the side window. The edge of the road dropped off into a steep canyon. She closed her eyes. If the end was about to hit her, she didn't want to see it coming. Sharp curves threw her body first one way against the car door, then in the other direction. She tightened the shoulder strap on her seat belt. Then another sharp turn and the sound of gravel. They had left the paved road. They bumped and bounced on the dirt road, occasionally spinning a tire in the mud. A bit of relief settled inside her. Their four-wheel drive would take them places their pursuer couldn't go. She kept her eyes closed as the minutes ticked away.

The sharp curves and the frantic ride calmed down. She could tell from the sound and the feel that they were back on a paved road. She opened her eyes, first one and finally both of them. She recognized their location. They were on the road leading into the area where his cabin was. About ten minutes later they turned onto the fire road, then pulled into his carport. She took a deep breath, held it a few seconds, then slowly exhaled.

"Are you all right?" His voice broke the silence. It was the first either of them had spoken since turning onto the mountain road. "Or perhaps a better question might be to ask if your nerves have settled down yet." A slight grin pulled at the corners of his mouth. "At least you have your eyes open again."

She slowly shook her head as she unfastened her seat belt. "If I don't end up with some bruises from this seat belt, I'll be surprised. There's not a roller coaster in the world that can equal the ride we just took. I can truthfully say I was terrified."

"We definitely lost whoever was following us. And it's just possible that right now he's mired down in the mud or he might even have torn out the undercarriage of his car on some rocks. Either way, I'd say he's on foot and isn't even sure of where he is, which is going to make it difficult for him to call someone on his cell phone and give them directions for picking him up."

She was finally able to muster a smile in an attempt to project a confident manner. If only she actually felt that calm. "Assuming he can even get a signal for his cell phone."

They climbed out of the car and hurried inside the cabin. Reece locked the cabin door, then pulled off his boots and hung his jacket on the coat hook. He caught the hint of uneasiness that crossed Brandi's face as she shrugged out of the rain jacket he had given her to wear. He took it from her and hung it next to his as she took off her muddy shoes.

"Are you all right?" Perhaps he had misjudged the situation. She might have been more shaken than he realized. "I have to admit that it was a pretty wild ride over the back roads, but we lost whoever was following us."

She looked up at him, a hint of apprehension lingering on her features. "Are you sure?"

He tentatively pulled her into his arms, as much an attempt to comfort her as it was a desire to hold her. "Absolutely."

His confident manner provided a sense of calm for her rattled nerves. "I'm fine." She mustered a slight smile. "It was a bit of a harrowing experience, but certainly not compared to being abducted."

He was more than aware that she had not made any

attempt to step back from his embrace. Did he dare push for more? The last thing he wanted to do was make her uneasy about being alone with him in the cabin all night. Then he felt her arms circle around his waist. He cradled her head against his shoulder, aware of her trembling body pressed against his.

They stood entwined in each other's arms, savoring the closeness—two people, each dealing with a personal inner turmoil and tentatively reaching out for comfort. It was finally Brandi who intruded into the rapidly escalating emotional intimacy of the moment. She stepped back from him, a hint of embarrassment darting across her face.

Reece quickly recovered his composure, turning the reality to the business at hand. "We've made some headway. We know for sure that Frank James is involved and apparently whatever is going on is somehow connected to those pictures you took—the missing negatives and prints."

Brandi didn't know whether she felt relief or disappointment at his businesslike attitude. "If I sit down with my appointment book and PDA, I can probably determine exactly where I was on which days. I've been trying to spend a couple of days each week on photography for my book rather than taking pictures several days in a row, so I should be able to figure out where I was on the last day I took pictures before the stalking started."

Her voice dropped off to a near whisper. "Assuming it was that day's photography that prompted the stalking."

"Is there any way those specific pictures can be reproduced? You said negatives and prints, so obviously they weren't digital and downloaded into your computer."

He studied her face. His goal was Frank James, but he could not deny his intense attraction to Brandi. He wanted to hold her in his arms again, to comfort her obvious fears. However, he didn't want her to get the wrong impression and become fearful of the circumstances that had them hidden in his cabin. "I don't suppose there's any possibility that you might have scanned them into your computer?"

"No, but that's a good suggestion for the future as a backup."

"Did you show the pictures to anyone? Did you make additional copies of any of those pictures and give them to someone?"

She took a couple of steps back from him in an effort to put some distance between her and the sensual pull of his masculinity. She flashed on the moment in the car when he had protectively covered her body with his and the sensation of being wrapped in the comfort and security of his strong arms.

A curious look of contemplation covered her features. "A couple of weeks ago I printed a random sampling and sent them to my agent to show her the type of pictures I had in mind, but I don't recall exactly which ones I sent...or precisely which day I sent them. I would have referenced the negative number on my file copy of the letter, but without the individual negatives I couldn't be sure which ones they were, although the reference number would have included the date that the picture was taken. That would, at least, tell me if any of the pictures I sent her were among those I took a month ago."

"Okay, here's what I want you to do right now."

He noticed the way she tried to stifle a yawn. He glanced at his watch and noted that it was almost three o'clock in the morning. "Correction. Make that first thing after we've gotten some sleep."

It had been a long day for him, and for her it had been both long and harrowing, starting off with being abducted. In addition to being physically tired, she had to be emotionally drained. A moment of anxiety darted through him. It couldn't be put off any longer. They both needed to get some sleep.

He awkwardly shifted his weight from one foot to the other. He had been doing his best to maintain a safe distance from her. Other than a couple of slips, he had been doing an admirable job of it, considering how much her nearness pulled and tugged at his desires. How much longer would the burning desire continue to churn inside him?

And how much longer would he be able to ignore it?

"I...uh, I think we should go to bed. And you haven't had an opportunity to take that shower yet." Reece nervously cleared his throat. "I want you to know...well, I think you'll agree that it would be best if you stayed here tonight rather than us venturing out again to find you a motel room somewhere. Whoever was following us might still be searching the main roads in hopes of spotting my car. Besides, we have lots of work to do. We can't afford the time it takes to travel back and forth."

The nervous tension churned in the pit of his stomach. It was a fine line between doing what he knew was best for all concerned and wanting to kiss her again—this time with all the passion coursing through his body.

It was more than just sex, more than the need to fulfill his pent-up urges. It had been a long time since he had held a woman—stroked her hair, caressed her shoulders, felt the texture of her skin, tasted the sweetness of her mouth. All the little nuances that enhanced sex with someone special. And it wasn't just that it had been a long time since he had been with a woman. Brandi wasn't just some woman who had happened across his path.

There was truly something very special about her, something he wanted to know much better. Then a more pragmatic thought shoved the others aside. Once again he found himself up against Frank James. Was this Cindy Thatcher all over again? Was he allowing himself to be led down the garden path with disaster waiting just around the bend?

He saw the vulnerability etched into her features and it pulled at his emotions. She needed his help. He brushed his fingertips against her cheek, then pulled her into his embrace. He held her, but not too tightly. The last thing he wanted to do was make her fearful of what the night would bring or cause her any unwarranted anxiety due to their unusual circumstances. He felt her hesitation, then she slipped her arms around his waist as she had done before.

He threaded his fingers through the silky strands of her hair, then cradled her head against his shoulder. The calm flowed through his body, the type of calm he hadn't experienced in a long time. She felt so good in his arms, as if she belonged there. He pressed his lips to her forehead and continued to hold her. Neither of them said anything for several seconds. Then he placed his fingertips beneath her chin and lifted until her face turned up toward his. He wasn't sure what he saw in her eyes, but he knew it wasn't fear or trepidation. He lowered his head, hesitated, then brought his mouth down on hers.

It was a kiss as much of tenderness and concern as it was one of heated passion. His kiss deepened. He tightened his embrace, pulling her body closer to him. He caressed her shoulders and back. Her response, at first tentative, increased in fervor as the kiss continued.

Brandi wasn't sure exactly what to do. The situation was, to say the least, very unusual. She felt sure that if she asked he would drive her to a motel. She also knew it was not the most expedient thing for them to do. Reece had been correct. Whoever had tried to follow them from her house could easily spot them if they ventured out onto the main road into an area populated enough to have a motel.

And the bottom line was that she didn't want to leave.

She may have known what she didn't want, but she wasn't at all sure exactly what she *did* want. But somewhere in that confusion she knew she would find Reece Covington. Then all her thoughts stopped the moment his tongue probed between her lips.

Her pulse raced and her heart pounded. Only this time it wasn't fear. She welcomed his tongue as it twined with hers. The excitement rippled through her body. The fog began to lift from her confusion, revealing what she had been trying to deny. It was Reece Covington she wanted. But here and now? The prospect frightened her.

It was too much and was definitely too soon.

She broke off the kiss. A nervous anxiety jittered through her reality. Her words came out as a breathless whisper. "This is too fast. I don't really know you." She shook her head. It was more an involuntary gesture than a conscious act. "These circumstances..."

Disappointment flooded through him, but he knew she was right. He released her from his embrace. He took a steadying breath in an attempt to quell his uneasiness. Had he acted too rashly? Pushed her too far, especially considering the circumstances? He didn't know.

"Give me a few minutes to get some clean clothes along with a pillow and blankets, then you can have the bedroom for the night. You'll find clean towels and washcloths in the bathroom cupboard."

"I feel guilty taking your bedroom away from you. I can sleep on the sofa."

"No. I insist that you take the bedroom. The door doesn't lock, but you can prop a chair under the doorknob if it will make you feel more comfortable..." A tremor of anxiety attached itself to his words. "More secure."

One final look of desire passed between them before they went their separate ways to get ready for bed.

Chapter Five

Morning was half over before Reece woke. The bedroom door was still closed. He took a quick shower, shaved, dressed, then went to the kitchen and made coffee. He stared at the contents of the refrigerator, trying to decide what to do about breakfast. He finally grabbed a bottle of orange juice and set it on the counter.

"That coffee sure smells good."

He whirled around and saw Brandi framed in the kitchen door. He hadn't seen her between the time she'd showered, then disappeared into the bedroom. The sight nearly took his breath away. Her short blond hair feathered softly around her face. The scratches on her face were less noticeable than they had been the day before when they had been fresh. In fact, her skin almost glowed. She was the most beautiful woman he had ever seen—a natural beauty that didn't need any enhancement.

It took a moment before he finally found his voice. "Good morning. Did you sleep well? You look rested."

A slight flush of embarrassment covered her cheeks. "Yes, I feel much better. I appreciate you giving up your bedroom for me."

"No problem. The sofa bed is comfortable enough."

He grabbed two coffee mugs, filled them and handed one of them to her. "Do you need cream or sugar?"

"No, this is fine just the way it is." Idle, polite chitchat. She didn't know whether to categorize it as mindless conversation that covered her uncertainty or an awkward embarrassment over what could very easily have happened last night. And if truth be known, to which she wouldn't have put forth much of an objection had he chosen to pursue it.

"I was just wondering what to do about breakfast, especially since it's after ten o'clock. I got as far as coffee and orange juice. What would you like? I can fix some bacon and eggs. I also have cereal if you'd rather have that."

"Please, don't go to any trouble for me. Some juice and maybe a piece of toast will be fine. I'm not much of a cereal person."

"Then bacon and eggs it is. That should hold us until dinnertime. Will scrambled be okay?"

She sipped her coffee and watched as he prepared breakfast. He seemed to have stepped into the role of both her protector and caretaker. She didn't really want a protector, per se. She wanted…she *needed*… someone to help her, but she didn't want someone to fight her battle for her or take care of her as if she were some helpless little waif. But she'd felt so safe in the security of his embrace. She shook away the unwanted thought.

"Let me help you with that." She busied herself setting the table.

They ate quickly, then turned their attention to the business at hand.

"I want you to call your agent and have her scan the pictures into her computer, then e-mail them as a zip file attachment. She should e-mail them to you, not me. You can access your e-mail from my computer. Then I want you to sit down with your appointment book and PDA and figure out exactly where you were taking pictures just before the stalking began. In fact, see if you can pinpoint the locations for the two weeks prior to the onset of the stalking. And while you're doing that, I'm going to make a couple of phone calls and see if I can get us some outside help."

"Outside help? From whom? We can't trust any of the local police, especially anyone in Rocky Shores. We have no way of knowing who might be working with Frank James. Do you think it will be safe to talk to someone at the state level?"

"I had someone a little higher up in mind—an FBI agent who owes me a couple of favors, not the least of which is that I saved his life when I was involved in a case he was working on a few years ago."

"Do you trust him?"

"Enough to contact him, but I won't be giving him full details. I won't reveal your identity or the exact nature of the problem."

Reece took his two cell phones off the chargers where they had been overnight. "I noticed that you don't have a cell phone."

"I do, but it's in my car. I had placed it on the passenger seat just before I was abducted."

Reece furrowed his brow into a slight frown. "We should have grabbed it when we were there last night."

"Do we dare go back to get it?"

"Hmm...now that I'm thinking about it, it's just as well that we don't have it. I'm sure Frank has already obtained your cell phone number and is monitoring any possible use. I have two cell phones. There's the one I use most of the time and a second one I reserve for special circumstances. As with the cabin and my car, registration of the numbers is hidden behind a barrage of obstacles that will make it very difficult to trace the location of this cabin through my cell phone numbers."

He handed her one of the cell phones. "Here. Use this to call your agent with the instructions for sending us the pictures. But first I want to get you a photograph of Frank James." He turned on his laptop computer. After a couple of minutes he had the personnel files of the Rocky Shores Police Department on the screen.

Brandi looked over his shoulder. "That's not their Web site. Did you hack into their computer system?"

He shot her a sly look and a wink. "Don't be ridiculous. That would be illegal."

He pulled up the department ID picture of Frank James. "Is this the man who abducted you?"

A cold tremor shuddered through her body as she stared at the face. "Yes, that's the man. I'm sure of it."

"I thought so. Frank James...the police detective who planted evidence and lied on the witness stand, resulting in my conviction and two-year prison term."

She heard the bitterness and anger in his voice. She didn't know specifically why he had been sent to prison or the exact circumstances surrounding his arrest, but she knew he would tell her when the time was right. And despite her initial doubts, she also believed he was innocent, just as he had claimed. She had never been in a position before where she needed to put blind faith in anyone, especially a stranger…a man she barely knew.

But she trusted him, even though she couldn't explain why.

Reece did a quick scan of Frank's file. "Look…" He pointed to the screen. "It says he has an allergy to penicillin. That fits in with the medical alert bracelet you saw."

He continued to stare at the picture of Frank James. He clenched his jaw, setting his features into a hard line of determination. Then he abruptly shut down the computer and rose from the chair, his attitude once again all business. "While you're calling your agent, I'm going to get us that help I mentioned."

Brandi sat at his desk as she placed the call. Reece took the other cell phone that he used for special circumstances and walked out onto the front porch of the cabin. He dialed the number. The familiar voice finally came on the line.

"Hodges."

"Joe…it's Reece Covington."

There was a long pause before Joe responded, his voice noticeably hesitant. "Reece…well, this is a surprise. It's been a long time."

"It's been over two years."

"Yes…before you were…uh…"

"Before I went to prison. Is that what you're trying

not to say?" Something about Joe's tone of voice, a reticence in his attitude, put Reece on alert. "I have a *situation* and I could use your assistance."

"Situation? What type of situation?"

"I have a—" he paused a moment, not sure how to categorize Brandi "—a *friend* who is in desperate need of help. As you probably know, going to prison cost me my private investigator's license—at least for the time being. I can't legally take on a client, charge a fee and work a case. And needless to say, I'm not allowed to have any firearms—concealed or otherwise."

"So, what is it you want from me? I have a job. I'm an FBI agent, not a private eye looking for my next client."

"I want to meet with you so I can give you some information about my friend's problem. I think you can be helpful in resolving the situation."

"Why don't you take it to the local police?"

"I can't. They're part of the problem."

"Whose jurisdiction is it?"

"Rocky Shores."

"I see. Well..."

Reece's muscles tensed in an involuntary response to Joe's hesitation and his tone of voice. "Do I need to put this on the basis of calling in the *favor* you owe me?"

"No, of course not. I was just looking at my schedule to see what would be a good time. Where are you?"

"Where I am is unimportant. What matters is where and when we can meet."

"Okay. How about in half an hour at Pike Place Market?"

"No good. I have some other business to take care of first. How about lunch at the Space Needle? You make the reservation." Reece had no intention of confiding to Joe that he was not actually in Seattle and couldn't possibly be at the designated location in half an hour.

"All right. Is one o'clock okay?"

"Make it one-thirty." Reece disconnected the call without bothering to say goodbye. He had already been on the call longer than he wanted to be. A nagging hint of apprehension continued to linger in the back of his mind. He knew he could attribute part of Joe's attitude to his surprise at hearing from him after all this time and especially under the circumstances. But there was something else that he couldn't define.

He turned as he heard Brandi walk out onto the porch. "Were you able to reach your agent? Will she be able to scan the pictures into her computer?" He escorted her back inside, not wanting her to remain exposed to the possibility of prying eyes…just in case.

"Yes, but she was just walking out the door when the phone stopped her. She won't be able to do it until tomorrow. She'll send them as soon as they're ready."

"I'm meeting with Joe at one-thirty this afternoon. I want you to stay here."

"I won't be going with you? But wouldn't he want to meet me and hear the story from me if he's going to help us?"

"I'm sure that's exactly what he would want, but that's not what he's going to get. I'm not exposing you to unnecessary danger. I do not intend, at least not at this point in time, to reveal your identity to Joe…or to anyone else for that matter."

She wrinkled her brow in confusion. "I thought you said you trusted this guy, that you saved his life so he owes you."

"I also haven't seen or talked to him since I ended up in prison. I told him I was innocent at the time of my arrest—" a bittersweet chuckle escaped his lips "—but I guess that's what everyone says." There was no mistaking the sarcasm that had surrounded his words.

"So, that makes this a whole new ballgame where we need to re-establish the ground rules. And then there's the other consideration. I certainly don't want you to be someplace where you could be spotted by Frank or one of his cohorts. Since we don't know who else is involved other than Frank, we have no way of knowing who to be on the lookout for."

"How much do you plan to tell your FBI friend?"

"Just the bare facts—that you're being stalked by Frank James—and see what kind of reaction I get to that. If he seems receptive and willing to help, then I'll tell him more. Hopefully we'll be able to get some information from Joe about the activities of Frank James and who his associates are, especially who would be a likely candidate for the person that Frank reports to as far as his *extracurricular activities* are concerned."

Her eyes widened in surprise. "You mean Frank isn't the boss?"

"I'd be surprised if he was. My opinion of Frank James says that if he were the top dog, he would have eliminated you without giving it a second thought. Obviously someone else is making the ultimate decisions or you wouldn't be alive. And whoever it is, it's someone who has more clout than Frank does and that's a name I hope Joe can provide to us."

She wrinkled her brow into a contemplative frown. "Do you think he reports to some sort of crime boss?"

"I don't know. It's either that or someone *official* who's higher up than he is, someone with dirty hands who has a lot more power than Frank. Either way, it's information we need if we're going to figure out what's happening and how to put a stop to it."

She bit at her lower lip, a nervous gesture that belied her attempt to project a confident and secure appearance. "Are we talking about some kind of conspiracy? Something I know, something I saw, something I heard… something I somehow became involved in that no one was supposed to know about?"

He allowed a slight scowl. "I don't know. I'm not sure exactly what we're dealing with, but that's definitely a possibility. Whatever it is, I intend to get to the bottom of it." *And take Frank James down in the process, make him pay for what he did to me.* Then a more pressing reality entered his mind, one that managed to overshadow his thoughts of personal revenge.

He pulled Brandi into his arms and held her body tightly against his. He tenderly stroked her hair while reveling in her closeness. All the heated passion and tender feelings he had wanted to explore last night flooded his consciousness. *And I also want him to pay for what he's doing to you.*

Brandi slipped her arms around his waist as she rested her head against his shoulder. She felt so safe when he held her, as if nothing bad could ever touch her. It had been less than twenty-four hours since she first set eyes on him, but it seemed as if they had packed years of closeness into those hours. Yes, she trusted this man—trusted him with her life. A fleeting thought questioned whether those were prophetic words that would come back to haunt her, words that would be put to the test. She shoved the unwelcome thought aside as she drew from his strength.

Then his mouth came down on hers, a mouth that mingled tenderness with a heated passion.

The kiss ended all too soon. No one had ever kissed her the way he did. No one had ever stirred her desires the way he did. No one had ever made her want to jump in bed for a night of no-strings-attached lovemaking the way he did.

REECE ARRIVED AT THE Space Needle half an hour early so he could check out the area. He saw Joe Hodges arrive but waited to see what would happen. When he was satisfied that Joe had come alone, he made his appearance. He held out his hand toward the FBI agent, who clasped it in a firm handshake.

"Joe...it's good to see you again. You're looking well." Reece extended an outwardly pleasant smile while remaining constantly alert to everything going on around him.

"It's been a long time, Reece. I must say, you're looking none the worse for wear from your...uh, *vacation* at the state's expense."

Reece narrowed his eyes as he paused to appraise the man standing in front of him. "Yes, my *unfortunate incarceration.*"

A moment of awkward silence invaded the space between them before the elevator door opened. They went up to the restaurant and were seated at one of the window tables with the ever-changing view as the restaurant made its hourly 360-degree revolution.

They exchanged meaningless pleasantries, commented on the weather and basically engaged in mindless chitchat for a few minutes until after the waiter had taken their orders. Then Joe leaned forward, dropped his voice to a low tone and became all business.

"All right, what's this situation you mentioned and what do you want from me?"

Reece had always liked that about Joe, the way he cut through everything and got right to the point. He liked the directness. He didn't have the time or the desire to jockey for position, play the little ego games that he found to be a waste of time.

He fixed Joe with a steady gaze, prepared to catch even the slightest inflection in response to what he was about to say. "You know Frank James, don't you? Detective Lieutenant Frank James of the Rocky Shores Police Department?" He caught a quick look of something that flickered through Joe's eyes, but disappeared before he could read it.

"I met him once. A casual acquaintance of mine introduced us at a social gathering. What does he have to do with this?"

He saw the wariness dart across Joe's face, then disappear as quickly as it had appeared. Joe was playing it cagey, but in all fairness it was no different than what he would do if someone put him in the same position.

"My friend that I mentioned is being stalked by Frank." He was careful not to mention whether he was talking about a man or a woman, preferring to leave Brandi as someone gender neutral for the time being.

Joe leaned back in his chair, his voice and body language signaling a finality to the topic of conversation. "If the Rocky Shores Police Department has someone under surveillance—"

"The police don't have my friend under surveillance. My friend attempted to report the stalking to them before knowing who was involved, but they blew it off and treated the information as if it had come from some neurotic nutcase—didn't even do a report on it. It turns out that Frank is the stalker. He's broken into my friend's house, stolen some personal property and has gone so far as to carry out an abduction in the middle of the day. My friend managed to escape and has gone into hiding."

Joe's reaction to this bit of information was immediate and intense. His body jerked to attention, and he leaned forward again after giving a quick glance around to see if anyone was within earshot.

"How do you know this? Who is this *friend* of yours?"

"I know this because my friend told me about the stalking and abduction. I looked into it—in an *unofficial* capacity, of course—and who do you suppose I found right in the middle of things? None other than Frank James."

Joe furrowed his brow into a contemplative scowl. "But why would a decorated police detective do that?"

Reece leaned back in his chair, a smirk of satisfaction tugging at the corners of his mouth. "Ah...now you've arrived at the crux of the problem. Why, indeed, would Frank James be doing such a terrible thing to my friend?"

"That smug expression tells me you already know the answer."

"I don't know the answer, at least not all of it."

The waiter arrived with their food, bringing the conversation to an abrupt halt. Reece took advantage of the interruption and used it to play on Joe's curiosity and nerves. He could tell he had hooked the FBI agent, and now he needed to reel him in. From his experience with Joe, the surest way to accomplish that was to change the subject. If Joe brought it up again within the next five minutes, he knew he would get the cooperation he wanted.

Reece set about eating his lunch, making the occasional comment on the quality of the food, the recent rainstorm and the gathering storm clouds that hung low on the horizon, indicating another bout of heavy rain coming in off the Pacific Ocean. And all the while he kept a careful eye on Joe, monitoring his body language for any hint of what was going through his mind. He didn't like playing games, but this wasn't a game. It was serious business.

Deadly serious.

And the safety of someone who was growing more special by the minute was at stake. Someone who had managed to put a shift in his priorities, a subtle realization that surprised him. Stopping Frank James was still his goal, but now it was more about protecting Brandi than it was the personal matter of settling a score.

"So...what is it you want from me?"

Joe tried to sound casual, but his attempt failed miserably. An inner spark of satisfaction told Reece that he had Joe's cooperation—at least to a point. He leaned forward, his voice dropping to a conspiratorial level. He fixed Joe with a hard stare, showing that he was all business and very determined.

"I want to know if there's anything in federal files about Frank James, any little irregularities connected with his job performance. Any suspicions of wrongdoing or criminal activity. Frank is involved in a ton of illegal stuff. I know that for a fact. He's the one who lied on the witness stand and fit the frame around me with the help of a sexy little vixen with incredible acting skills...along with her other many talents. I'm convinced that someone higher up than Frank is calling the shots, but I don't know who. It could be someone in a position of legal authority, someone with political clout or someone walking the other side of the fence. Either way, Frank James is a dirty cop and has to be taken down."

Joe leaned back in his chair, a troubled expression crossing his features as he emitted a low whistle. "You're not asking for much, are you? As far as I can tell, there's nothing here that officially involves any federal agency, which means the FBI can't be involved in local matters unless the police invite us in. You say your friend was abducted but escaped. Since your friend didn't report the abduction, there's no official record that it even happened. I can see why you don't want to take it to the Rocky Shores police since you believe that Frank James is somehow involved. But what about—"

"Frank is not merely a...what is that expression you are using now—*person of interest*...someone who is *somehow involved.* He's definitely in the middle of whatever it is that's going on. He didn't abduct my friend simply because it was a slow day and he didn't have anything better to do."

"What do you think is going on? Without proof what do you expect anyone to do? Why haven't you taken this to someone on the state level?"

"Nope, I can't take a chance. I don't know anyone on that level well enough, and they don't know me that well, either. And then there's my record, which shows I was just released after two years in prison and that Frank James was the prosecution's chief witness against me. That certainly doesn't give me any credibility against a decorated police lieutenant."

"I'd like to meet with your friend, hear the story first-hand."

"Perhaps at some time in the future, but not now."

"You're not even going to tell me who this friend of yours is?"

"No—not at this time."

"So, what you're saying is that I'm supposed to help you, but you aren't going to trust me."

Reece allowed a hint of a teasing grin. "It does sound that way, doesn't it?"

Joe slowly shook his head, his brow knitted in concentration. He drew in a deep breath, held it for a moment, then exhaled in a sigh of resignation. "Okay. I can't make any promises, but I'll see if I can find something…maybe make a few discreet inquiries of other agencies in addition to checking our files."

"That's all I'm asking." Reece jotted his cell phone number on a napkin and handed it to Joe. "You can reach me through this number. Don't bother trying to run it down to find a location on me because it won't lead you anywhere."

Joe took the napkin and shoved it in his pocket as a slight grin turned the corners of his mouth. "You always were very cautious. Makes me wonder how you allowed yourself to be in a position where you could be framed and end up in prison."

He could see that Joe was baiting him, looking for an impulsive comment that might divulge some information. But Reece kept his thoughts carefully in check. He did not intend to give Joe that much satisfaction.

The two men finished their lunch, their conversation turning to more generic matters. When the check came, Reece handed it to Joe along with a sly grin.

"Here, you have a job and an expense account. I'm just a humble out-of-work ex-private eye trying to get my life back together."

Joe chuckled appreciatively and accepted the check. "I sincerely doubt that things are as dire for you as you make them sound."

Somewhere in the back of his mind Reece couldn't

shake the feeling that he had been right in not trusting Joe with Brandi's identity. But had he made a colossal mistake in contacting Joe? The possibility weighed heavily on his mind.

Chapter Six

Following lunch with Joe Hodges, Reece took care of some shopping necessities before returning to the cabin—printer ink and paper, a new software program for his computer, some clothing items and a couple of bottles of wine. Then he collected his mail from the private company that provided post office boxes. He checked his watch. By the time he got back to the cabin it would be almost five o'clock. Nearly dinnertime.

And then another night spent sleeping under the same roof with Brandi Doyle. Another night of testing his ability to keep his needs and desires in tight control. Another night of wanting to hold her in his arms. Another night of wanting to shut out the rest of the world and its problems. Another night of wanting to make passionate love to the most exciting woman he had ever met. Another night of knowing that he couldn't take advantage of the unusual circumstances or her vulnerability.

Another night of knowing that he could not compromise the trust she had placed in him.

Myriad thoughts and feelings circulated through his

mind as he drove to his cabin. Even though Joe Hodges had promised to help, his conversation had left Reece uneasy. Nothing specific, just a feeling that Joe was hiding something relevant from him, that he was holding back on some information. It had reinforced his decision to keep Brandi's identity a secret and not mention what they had discovered so far.

He pulled into the carport, grabbed his purchases and hurried into the cabin.

He called to Brandi. "I'm back."

"I'm in the kitchen."

He set his computer supplies on his desk, then went to his bedroom to put away his other purchases. He proceeded to the kitchen carrying the bottles of wine. He paused at the door and watched her for a moment. The way she moved, the curve of her hip, the way her sweater caressed her breasts—everything about her tugged at his libido. But there was more than lustful desire. There was also the way she felt in his arms, the sense of contentment he experienced when he was with her, the feeling of settled calm she brought to his life in spite of the external turmoil that currently surrounded them.

He set the bottles of wine on the counter, then walked up behind her and impulsively wrapped his arms around her waist. He nuzzled the side of her neck as he turned her around within his embrace until she faced him. He searched the depths of her eyes, looking for any hint of what she wanted. Any clue to what he should do and how he should proceed.

Or, more accurately, *if* he should proceed at all.

His desires won out over his uneasiness. He captured her mouth with a kiss that started out tender, but quickly escalated. Without hesitation, she raised her arms around his neck and met his kiss with a passion of her own.

The entire time he'd been gone, her thoughts had jumped back and forth between two extremes. Her first thought had been the need for them to return to her house again. They had been interrupted and made their escape before she had been able to finish searching her files to see what else was missing besides the recent location pictures for her book. Her other thought had centered around what that night would bring. Sleeping in his bed while knowing he was just on the other side of the bedroom door had made for a frustrating night.

Though she barely knew him and wasn't even sure about the validity of everything he had told her, she had still made the decision to trust him based primarily on gut instinct. Her life had been turned upside down and inside out, then suddenly this mysterious stranger had appeared. She had opened her eyes and there he'd been—literally. It had taken only a few hours for her to realize he was the most exciting and desirable man she had ever met. But was it merely the circumstances that made him seem so? Had the unusual nature of their relationship and the danger surrounding them made it seem as if they needed to grab what they could before it was too late?

The entire time she was being stalked, she'd felt as if she had almost no control over her own life. Just when everything had seemed the bleakest, this handsome stranger had suddenly materialized. Almost like the proverbial cavalry coming to the rescue at the last minute, just in time to save the wagon train. But how much of what she felt for him was real—and how much an illusion that gave her some hope to hold on to?

Her thoughts turned again to the need for them to go back to her house and finish their search. Then the sensation of his tongue teasing her lips chased the practical thoughts from her mind. She opened her mouth to accept his probing tongue. The longing flowed through her body. She twined her fingers through his thick hair. Was it the heightened tension of the situation? The adrenaline surge from the danger? There was nothing normal, nothing ordinary about the circumstances that had brought them together. Things between them seemed to have moved at lightning speed. Was it too fast?

Any thought as to whether this was the right thing to be doing flew out the window. She wanted Reece Covington. She pressed her body against his.

A moment of panic hit Reece like a ton of bricks. Last night she had told him he was moving too fast. She had let him know she was uncomfortable with the growing physical contact between them. So exactly what did he think he was doing now? He broke off the kiss but couldn't quite bring himself to turn her loose. He drew in a steadying breath, then brushed a soft kiss against her forehead.

Last night had been a test of his ability to conduct himself properly, to maintain his distance while knowing that she was in his bed in the next room. He had passed the test. But would he be able to pass that test for a second night? Not that he would ever try to force himself on her, but was it possible that he had taken her vulnerability and mistaken it for encouragement? The thoughts continued to circulate through his mind—thoughts that were part desire and part worry.

"Reece...I, uh..."

Her words broke into his thoughts. Something about the timbre of her voice set him on alert. He reluctantly released her from his embrace. "Yes?"

"I've been thinking and...well, I've given it quite a bit of thought...and, uh..." She held several seconds of eye contact with him. She had weighed the choices and had finally come to a decision. "I think we need to make another trip to my house."

Her words caught him completely off guard. He saw the concern in her eyes, but that didn't lessen his reaction to what she had said even though it was obvious that she was uncomfortable with the topic. He tried, but he couldn't keep the slight edge out of his voice, a combination of disbelief and agitation.

"You want to go back to take another look through your house? Why? Is there something specific you need? Can't we just buy whatever it is at a store somewhere?"

"Well, uh...we were interrupted before I could finish searching through my files to see if I could tell what was missing. We know the negatives and prints of my recent location pictures were taken, but I don't know if all of them were missing or only the recent ones. The first few months' worth of pictures weren't with the ones that we know are missing."

He frowned as he turned over this new bit of information in his mind. "Do you realize how risky that would be? Why didn't you mention this earlier?"

"It didn't occur to me until a little while ago." A barely audible sigh escaped her lips as a look of anguish crossed her face. "It's just that everything has happened so fast. My mind is almost a blur. One moment I'm getting into my car to go to the grocery store and the next thing I know I'm frightened nearly out of my mind and running for my life in an attempt to get away from my abductor."

A sob caught in her throat. She tried to hide it but knew she had not been very successful. The last thing she wanted to do was fall apart. "I needed to be able to step back from it for a few hours and find a sanctuary where I could try to put everything together so that it made sense. You've given me that by allowing me to stay here. I truly appreciate your kindness and consideration, but I'm still trying to fit all the pieces together. I understand it intellectually. I know what's happening and what we need to do, but I'm having a difficult time absorbing it emotionally. Right now I feel like I don't have any control over my own life, and I don't like that feeling."

He heard her words and instantly understood exactly what she meant. It was the same thing he had gone through when outside forces had caused his life to spiral out of control and he'd ended up in prison. He knew he had to do whatever he could to help her regain that sense of control. If she wasn't able to restore that feeling of confidence in herself, then it would be a negative impact on her for the rest of her life. He had to do everything he could to help her.

"Okay. After dinner we'll return to your house so you can look through the rest of your files. Frank will probably assume that if we're going to return to your house we'd do it late at night or in the early morning hours before dawn. By doing it early in the evening we should avoid any type of interference from him."

She looked up at him. Her voice was a mere whisper, but he heard the sincerity and saw the relief in the depths of her eyes. "Thank you."

As sure as he was standing there he knew that she had managed to turn his priorities around by one hundred and eighty degrees. She was absolutely the top priority. What he didn't know was how he felt about it and whether she was even aware of the effect she had on him.

They had dinner, but he didn't open the bottle of wine. That would have to wait for another time, at the very least until after they had tackled the mountain roads again and concluded another foray into her house.

They set out for Rocky Shores. A little tingle of anxiety continued to churn in the pit of his stomach, enough to make sure his senses remained on alert. Regardless of what he had told her, he wasn't as sure about it himself. Frank James was not the type to leave a large hole in his surveillance. He might not be there personally, but there was a good chance that one of his men would be keeping an eye on her house, especially since he now knew someone had been there.

They were definitely taking a risk—a huge risk. But how could he say no to her, especially understanding her reasoning behind the request? If there was even a slight chance that they could find something that would help them resolve the mess she was in, then they had to do it. They had to take the chance.

Neither of them said much of anything on the drive to her house. The anxiety and trepidation that filled the air was thick enough to cut with a knife. He drove past her house, carefully scrutinizing everything that came across his line of sight. He drove up the alley, then down the next street where he had parked the previous night. When he was satisfied that everything was as it should be, he parked on the next street as he had done before, only this time with his car in front of the Gleasons' house in case they needed to cut through that yard again.

A few minutes later they entered her garage through the side door, then went inside the house. They proceeded directly to her office, where she started going through the older files.

FRANK JAMES WATCHED BRANDI'S home from his vantage point inside the vacant house across the street. She had obviously managed to find help somewhere. He didn't know the person's identity, but whoever it was had cleverly avoided surveillance. The man Brandi had helping her had given his cohort a dangerous pursuit through the mountains until finally losing him. Frank knew he needed to sharpen his tactics. Whoever was helping her knew exactly what he was doing and was very good at it.

In Frank's official capacity as a police detective, he had done a quick background check on her associates and close friends. There wasn't any name on the list who qualified. Whoever she had recruited was still a mystery to him.

He had grabbed her negatives and the prints. When he'd studied them, he'd found exactly what they feared might be there. But taking the evidence wasn't enough. They had to know if there were any other copies of the pictures, and if so, had she sent them to someone else. Even if she had no idea what she had captured on film, they could not take a chance on her discovering it later or someone else eventually figuring it out.

His *associate* had definitely put a scare into him. If he bungled it this time, he would need to do some fast talking to save his own neck. He had surprised someone at her house last night. There was a good chance that whoever it was would be returning to finish what he had started. And this time Frank would be ready. The mystery man would not escape him a second time.

He glanced at his watch. He had been sitting at the window in the vacant house for over two hours. Another hour and one of his men would be there to relieve him. He wanted twenty-four-hour surveillance on Brandi's house, but he only had a small group of trusted men he could pull from. He couldn't afford two men around the clock to watch the front and the back. In fact, he had short-changed his police duties to be able to devote more time to this little *problem.* Fortunately, her office was in the front of her house rather than the back. With the vacant house across the street, it made surveillance easier.

A quick flicker of light caught Frank's eye. He jerked

to attention. Someone was inside the house, specifically inside her office.

Frank left the vacant house, dashed crossed the street and made his way around to the back of Brandi's house.

"ANY LUCK?" REECE NERVOUSLY shifted his weight from one foot to the other as he watched Brandi.

"Everything is here, all the location pictures I shot several months ago. Apparently the only things missing are the more recent location photographs. We're at a dead end if the pictures I sent my agent weren't the specific ones they wanted. Without that, we'll never know why they were so important."

She let out a sigh of exasperation. "I guess that's it. I don't know where else to check or what else to look for. As near as I can tell, those specific negatives and prints are the only things missing." She grabbed her file copy of the letter she had sent her agent and shoved it in her purse.

They started to leave, making their way through the living room. A sound from the back of the house sent a hard jolt through Reece's body. He grabbed Brandi's arm, bringing her to an abrupt halt. He placed his finger to her lips, indicating that she should be quiet. They both stood very still, neither of them making a sound. Then he heard it again. Someone had entered the house.

Instinct took over. Reece shoved Brandi down to the floor behind the sofa, then positioned himself by the door, ready to intercept the intruder. He glanced toward the sofa. He felt confident in his ability to handle the intruder, even without having any type of a weapon. But he also had to protect Brandi. He couldn't allow anything to happen to her. He sucked in a calming breath, held it for several seconds, then slowly exhaled as he centered himself.

Even in the dark Reece immediately recognized the intruder as soon as he came through the door. So, Frank James had decided to handle this little problem personally. That was good and bad. It put him against an assailant whose capabilities he knew, but it also meant that he had to keep Frank from recognizing him. The last thing he wanted Frank to know was that he had become involved in Brandi's stalking and abduction.

Frank clicked off the safety of the Beretta .25-caliber semiautomatic pistol. As soon as he was fully inside the living room, Reece grabbed him from behind.

"What the hell—" Frank didn't have a chance to finish the rest of his sentence. Reece wrapped his left arm around Frank's neck, and with his right he reached for Frank's pistol.

Frank's swiftness caught him by surprise, but he still managed to knock the weapon to the floor. The two men grappled for it, bumping into furniture and turning over an end table.

The adrenaline pumped through Reece's body. His heart pounded in his chest as he struggled with Frank. Everything was on the line. It was more than his personal safety. Brandi's life was also at stake.

The sounds assaulted Brandi's ears. A sick sensation churned in the pit of her stomach. Her muscles tensed. She didn't know what to do. Her first thought was to jump up and try to help Reece, then she reined in the impulse. That was the last thing she should do. That would only give him more to worry about rather than being helpful.

Then the terrifying sound of a gunshot exploded around her. A cry of pain followed the sound of the shot, then an eerie silence—a silence that lasted only a second even though it felt like an eternity. Her breath froze in her lungs. Every muscle in her body twisted into tight knots.

She peered around the corner of the sofa, squinting to see through the darkness. One of the two men leaped to his feet and sprinted toward the back of the house and out the door. A moment later the other man scrambled to his feet. A million fears ran rampant through her body.

"Brandi—"

The sound of the familiar voice settled a calm over her shattered nerves. "Reece…are you all right? I heard a shot—"

The warmth of his touch stilled her words. He helped her up from the floor, then pulled her into his arms. He was safe. Nothing else mattered at that moment. She returned his embrace. His fingers twined in her hair, then he cradled her head against his shoulder. She felt the pounding of his heart. It matched her own racing pulse.

He took a calming breath. He didn't want to speak until he knew his voice would sound confident and controlled. "We need to get out of here right now. If the neighbors heard the shot, they could have called the police. That would give Frank the perfect excuse for being here—just answering the call because he was in the area."

He released her from his arms and stooped to pick up the pistol Frank had left behind, being careful to pick it up using his jacket sleeve to preserve Frank's fingerprints and keep from leaving any of his own. He put the pistol in his jacket pocket. He grabbed Brandi's hand, and they headed for the back door. He paused long enough to give a visual perusal to their escape route before going outside. They raced for his car and were soon on the way back to the cabin.

Reece kept a careful eye on his rearview mirror. He didn't detect anyone following them but still took the precaution of driving a circuitous route on a few back roads. They were almost to the cabin before he drew an easy breath. Apparently Frank had been alone and wasn't in a position to follow them.

Once they were inside, Reece locked the cabin door before turning on the lights. The sight of the blood smeared across the side of his jacket jumped out at Brandi. A startled gasp escaped her throat. A hard lump formed in her stomach, accompanied by a sick feeling that tried to make its way up her throat. She swallowed several times in an attempt to diminish the uncomfortable sensation. Her words came out as a frightened whisper.

"You've been shot—"

"No—I'm fine. Apparently Frank caught a piece of the bullet. That's his blood. It also explains why he didn't take the time to try and retrieve this before leaving the house." He grabbed a dish towel from the kitchen, then used it to pull Frank's pistol from his jacket pocket, making sure to handle it carefully. "This is a .25-caliber Beretta Bobcat semiautomatic pistol—small, lightweight and efficient. It's his personal property, not his officially issued weapon. He probably carries it in an ankle holster. The Rocky Shores Police Department uses 9 mm Glocks. If it had been his service weapon, he would have had to do a lot of explaining to account for it being missing." He released the magazine from the handle to check the number of bullets, then replaced it. He cleared the chamber. Only one shot missing. There were still seven shots remaining. He set the pistol on the desk.

Reece furrowed his brow in concentration. "I wonder if there are any unsolved cases with a ballistics match to this pistol." The words were more a matter of him thinking out loud than addressing the comments to Brandi.

"Then it was definitely Frank James you struggled with?"

"What?" Her question knocked him out of his thoughts. "Uh, yes. But I'm sure he didn't see my face. He had no way of knowing you were in the house or who I was."

"But wouldn't he have recognized me when we went inside?"

"I don't think he saw us enter the house. If he had, he would have been there much sooner or at the very least he would have called for someone to back him up before entering. We were ready to leave before he came in the back door. Since he didn't know who he was up against or how many people were actually inside the house, he did the only logical and prudent thing. He pulled a strategic retreat as soon as I disarmed him. I have no idea how badly he was wounded, but my guess is that he didn't hang around because he needed to get some medical help. There isn't enough blood on my jacket for his wound to have been very serious. However, even if it wasn't anything more than a flesh wound, he needed to stop the bleeding and clean the wound so it doesn't get infected."

Reece stared at Frank's pistol while turning several thoughts over in his mind. He grabbed the magnifying glass from the desk drawer, then turned on the lamp. He carefully inspected the surface of the weapon and also took close-up photographs. He made notes on a piece of paper—time and place of struggle, including the fact that some of Frank's blood would most likely be inside Brandi's house, Frank's fingerprints on the pistol, noticeable blow-back blood spray on the metal surface of the pistol and Frank's blood on Reece's jacket. If the bullet had caught only a small piece of his arm, then it was probably lodged in the floor or wall or a piece of furniture somewhere in Brandi's house. He removed his blood-stained jacket and put it with the note.

Brandi wrinkled her brow in confusion. "What are you doing?"

Reece glanced at her. "I'm documenting evidence for future reference. I need to test-fire this pistol in order to retrieve the spent cartridge with the ballistics markings. I also need the discarded shell casing." Then his voice trailed off, as if once again talking to himself rather than to Brandi. "But where and how to do it so that the bullet isn't destroyed by smashing into something solid." He immediately returned his full attention to the task at hand.

Then the light of realization struck him. He stared at Brandi without really seeing her. "The rain barrel! I can fire the shot into the water-filled rain barrel. The water would slow down the bullet to the point where it would sink through the water to the bottom of the barrel from its own weight rather than hit the bottom with full impact. The lands and grooves on the spent round would be preserved."

He glanced out the window. Should he do it now in the dark or wait until morning? He shook his head. He had to do it now, then hide the weapon in a secure location until he needed to produce it as evidence.

He turned toward Brandi and motioned toward the kitchen. "Grab that flashlight."

Reece carefully picked up the Beretta, again using the dish towel to preserve Frank's fingerprints and not leave any of his own. He walked out to the front porch with Brandi following closely behind him. The rain barrel stood at the corner next to the porch.

Reece carefully balanced on top of the porch railing so that he could get a direct downward shot into the water-filled barrel from a bit of a distance. He fired twice, then hopped down off the railing. A tingle of excitement raced through his body. It was a good feeling, one that told him he was accomplishing something positive. The energy flowing through him said they were moving closer to resolving her nightmare, recapturing his past and putting it straight.

Brandi handed him the flashlight so he could search the ground for the ejected casings. He retrieved them using a handkerchief and handed them to her wrapped in the handkerchief. "Don't touch these. Frank would have hand-loaded the cartridges into the magazine, so the casings should contain his fingerprints."

He paused as he stared into the rain barrel, then plunged his arm into the cold water. He felt around for the spent bullets. Finally, his fingers closed around the two objects and he pulled them out of the water.

He turned toward Brandi, his obvious pleasure beaming from his face. "Let's get inside where it's warm."

"Are you through with your experiment?"

"Yes, I have what I need."

They went inside, and Reece changed into a dry sweatshirt. Then he took the casings from Brandi and put the two spent cartridges with them. He took two envelopes from the desk and a piece of paper. He wrote the date, the make and model of the pistol and the serial number of the Beretta on the outside of both envelopes. He wrapped one casing in a tissue and one of the spent cartridges in another tissue, then placed them in one of the envelopes. On the piece of paper he wrote Brandi's name and address along with a brief chronology of events, starting with Brandi's abduction, including Frank's name and involvement. He added the tissue-wrapped cartridge and casing, then placed everything in the second envelope and sealed it. He set the envelopes to the side. Next he put the pistol inside his blood-stained jacket, rolled it up and placed it with the envelopes.

Reece pulled the desk away from the wall, then lifted up a couple of wooden planks, exposing the safe embedded in the concrete foundation beneath the cabin floor. He quickly worked the combination to open the safe. He hesitated for a moment, then removed a locked strongbox and set it on the table. Next, he placed the jacket and pistol inside the safe along with the envelope containing the full description of everything that had happened. He locked the safe and replaced the planks, then shoved the desk back in place.

Brandi gestured toward the items still on the table—the other envelope and the strongbox. "What are you going to do with those?"

"We need to be sure that we're covered and that any evidence we come across is well protected. Perhaps Joe Hodges can be of help in a new way. He should be able to get access to ballistics evidence from unsolved crimes. I'll give this envelope with a cartridge and casing to Joe. They show the ballistics markings of Frank's pistol, both the barrel lands and grooves on a spent cartridge and the firing pin imprint on the shell casing. If Joe can find a match connecting the pistol to an unsolved crime, it would be solid evidence against Frank for yet another crime in addition to your abduction."

He saw the worried expression on her face and heard the anxiety in her voice. "Do you trust Joe to get that type of information for you? What happens if he manages to somehow *lose* the bullet and casing?"

"That's one of the reasons I did two test firings. And, of course, I still have the pistol with the five remaining cartridges that contain Frank's fingerprints."

He furrowed his brow in momentary concentration. "Hmm...I think it would be a good idea if I sent the second envelope out of state to someone I trust, a P.I. friend who lives in California. What I want to avoid is firing all the rounds in the magazine. I want them preserved as much as possible."

"And what about that strongbox? What's inside it?"

Reece unlocked the box and withdrew a 9 mm semiautomatic pistol, the clip-on holster and two boxes of bullets. "I had this before I went to prison. They confiscated my legally registered weapons, but they didn't know about this one. It's been locked in the safe since before I went to prison. I took it out and cleaned it after I was released, then put it back since legally I'm not allowed to have any weapons anymore."

He sucked in a calming breath. "But that will change as soon as we get this mess cleared up and Frank is the one behind bars. I'll get my private investigator's license back along with my permit to carry a concealed weapon."

The look of despair that flashed across her face tugged at his emotions. He pulled her into his arms and held her. He wanted so much to provide her comfort and tell her not to worry, to be able to promise her that everything would be okay. He wanted to hold her long into the night, to share the warmth and give her his comfort.

He also knew it would be a very dangerous thing to do. He couldn't take advantage of her vulnerability or betray her trust regardless of what he wanted. He rested his cheek against the top of her head and closed his eyes. He continued to hold her, knowing that he should let go before he did something he would regret.

Brandi stepped back from the growing intimacy of his closeness. The warmth of his embrace had been a little *too* comfortable. The thought of spending the night securely wrapped in his arms a little *too* appealing. She could not deny how attractive she found him and how much she was physically drawn to him, but there was also the emotional aspect of the growing desire she felt for him. Another time and another place, then perhaps…

She took a calming breath in an attempt to steady her quivering insides. She looked up, capturing a moment of eye contact that did nothing to quell her growing desires.

"It…it's very late. Perhaps we should get some sleep."

He brushed his fingertips across her cheek as he gazed into the depths of her eyes. "I think you're right. It's been a long day."

The impulse was too strong, the desire too great. He lowered his head to hers and captured her mouth with a sizzling kiss that spoke volumes about the sensuality of the man. He left nothing hidden about exactly what was on his mind, but even as aroused as he was becoming he was careful not to push her. The last thing he wanted was for her to feel trapped, to comply with something she didn't really want because she felt as if she had no choice. If they made love, it would be because she wanted it as much as he did.

He felt her arms slip around his neck. Her response to his kiss raised his hopes, then she suddenly let go and stepped back. Confusion darted through him. Then he saw the apprehension in her eyes and knew he had gone too far. He wanted to say something but didn't know what to say that would somehow ease her mind and concerns.

"Brandi..."

"I'll see you in the morning."

She turned and walked into the bedroom, closing the door behind her. He stood motionless, staring at the closed bedroom door. A million thoughts and feelings raced through him, but none that he could specifically identify.

Or perhaps it was that he didn't want to identify them.

Chapter Seven

"Knock, knock. Anybody home?"

A startled Frank James jerked to attention at the sound of the voice. He looked up and saw Joe Hodges framed in his office door. He quickly replaced the receiver before he finished dialing, then rose from his chair. He leaned across his desk as he extended his hand toward his visitor. "Joe…this is a surprise. I haven't seen you since we worked together on the Peterson case. When was that—" he furrowed his brow in a moment of concentration "—a year ago? It was the same time that I trounced you at racquetball."

He flinched slightly as Joe Hodges grasped his hand. It was only a flesh wound on his upper arm, but Frank knew it would be sore for a couple of days. Fortunately, it hadn't needed the attention of a doctor, which would have required that the doctor report the gunshot wound. But the problem of having left his ankle pistol behind was another matter altogether, one that could be big trouble down the line if he didn't handle it carefully.

The two men shook hands, then Joe slid comfortably into the chair Frank had indicated. A soft chuckle escaped his throat. "I don't think the word *trounced* is appropriate. As I recall, the only reason you won was because of the cramp in my leg."

"Ah...you feds are all alike." Frank shot him a teasing grin. "You only acknowledge your own accomplishments and ignore it when someone else wins. I'll be happy to give you a rematch any time and any place you say."

Joe cocked his head and flashed a confident smile. "I have some time tomorrow. How about ten o'clock at the club?"

"Tomorrow isn't good for me. How long are you going to be around? I have some free time—" he made a show of checking his schedule "—day after tomorrow, late afternoon."

"You're on. Will four o'clock work for you?"

"Yes, great." Frank leaned back in his chair, not at all sure of how viable his arm would be. Hopefully it would have healed enough by then to not arouse any suspicion about his injury. "Now that we have the important stuff taken care of, what brings the FBI to my humble office?"

"Nothing in particular. I was in your neighborhood on another matter and thought I'd drop in and say hello. So, what's on your case load? Anything interesting?"

"Just the usual routine stuff...car theft, burglary, domestic violence involving a shooting."

"I'm working on a kidnapping case." Joe saw the immediate flicker of anxiety dart through Frank's eyes, but it disappeared as quickly as it had appeared.

Frank's body remained slightly tensed as he leaned

forward. "Kidnapping? Surely you don't mean here in Rocky Shores. I'm not aware of anyone here being grabbed." He realized he was talking too fast, his voice too intense. He tried to force a calm. "Nothing was reported to us."

"No, it doesn't have anything to do with Rocky Shores. The victim was abducted in Oregon and managed to escape in Bellevue. Having been taken across the state line from Oregon into Washington made it our jurisdiction. We believe the kidnappers were trying to take the victim out of the country and were on their way to Canada."

Frank leaned back, some of the tension visibly draining from his body. "I haven't heard anything about it. Are you keeping this under wraps for some reason?"

"Yes...for the time being. We haven't released any information about it to the media."

"Do you have any leads?"

"Nothing concrete...yet. Our biggest roadblock is a motive. The victim hasn't been able to shed any light on why he was grabbed."

"Not for money? That's usually the reason."

"There isn't any wealth involved, no real money to make the risk of a kidnapping worthwhile."

"Sounds like you have an interesting case. If there's anything I can help you with, give me a shout."

"Sure thing." Joe rose from his chair. "As long as I'm here, I should stop in and say hello to Lyle Hanover. I assume the D.A.'s office is next door in the courthouse building?"

"Yes, there's a connecting bridge between the buildings on the third floor. Let me give him a call, see if he's in his office. It will save you the trip in case he's in court right now."

"No need. If he's not there, I'll leave word with his secretary."

The two men shook hands and Frank watched as Joe left his office. As soon as the FBI agent was out of sight, Frank grabbed his phone and hit a speed-dial button.

A hint of urgency surrounded his words. "Joe Hodges was just in my office."

There was a moment's hesitation before a response traveled the phone line. "What does the FBI want with you?"

"He claimed it was just a social visit, that he was in the area, but I'm not so sure."

"What makes you wonder?"

"Well..." Frank tried to swallow his nervousness, hoping to keep it out of his voice. "There was someone in Brandi Doyle's house again last night. I'm still trying to run down the license plate of the vehicle from the night before last, but so far it's leading me in circles."

The long silence on the other end of the line told Frank what he didn't want to know—the man who ran the illicit activities, the man who called the shots, the man who ran Frank's extracurricular activities was not happy. It seemed like forever before he finally spoke.

"And you think the person in her house might have been Joe Hodges?"

"I don't know. I don't think so. The man in her house was bigger than Joe, but it's certainly a bothersome coincidence that Joe would show up in my office today."

A combination of shock and anger filled his cohort's voice. "You had your hands on this guy and let him get away? This makes two nights in a row that someone was in her house—two nights in a row that you let whoever it was get away from you."

"No. It's not like that. He…uh, from a distance he appeared larger than Joe." The last thing Frank wanted to do was admit that he had actually fought with the intruder with disastrous results and hadn't even gotten a look at his face.

"So what you're now telling me is that you stupidly grabbed the Doyle woman without permission, then you allowed her to escape, you twice lost someone who was in her house and now you're being visited by an FBI agent who may or may not be on to your activities." There was no mistaking the sarcasm. "Does that about sum it up?"

Frank was unable to keep the uneasiness out of his voice. "You're making it sound like a lot more than it is. There's no way she could identify me. She was blindfolded. And as for Joe…well, we go back a ways. It's not like some stranger from the FBI showing up at my office and interrogating me."

"She had to pull off that blindfold when she got loose and made her escape. She could have seen you then."

"No. I was inside paying for the gas."

"If she's gone to the FBI with this, then there's no way you'll be able to contain it and make it go away even with the agent being someone you know personally."

Frank put as much confidence into his voice as he could muster. "I'm sure there's nothing to worry about.

Joe didn't ask me any specific questions about anything. We talked for a few minutes and set a racquetball game for day after tomorrow at four o'clock. It was purely social, nothing more."

"You'd better be right, Frank. If not, well…I don't need to tell you what the consequences could be."

Frank terminated the conversation as quickly as possible, then returned to the problem he had been working on for the last twenty-four hours—tracking down the owner of the SUV that his man had chased from Brandi's house. It had been a frustrating search with lots of dead ends, but he knew he had to keep at it. The license plate was his only lead to the identity of the man helping Brandi.

Most likely the same man he had fought with the second night.

LYLE HANOVER'S INTERCOM buzzed. A moment later, Joe Hodges entered the assistant district attorney's office. Lyle rose from behind his desk and extended his hand.

"Joe—this is a pleasant surprise. What brings you here?"

"Just a social call. I'm here on another matter and thought I'd stop by and say hello to you and Frank. I just left his office."

"How's Frank doing? We used to occasionally get in a game of racquetball, but not any more."

"That's too bad. I thought you and Frank were personal friends in addition to working together."

"We are, but we've each been really busy lately and

haven't had an opportunity to get together socially. He's in the building just next door, but it seems that the only time I see him anymore is when it's a police matter and a case we're involved with."

"How's Frank doing? Any personal problems that you're aware of? I've been hearing rumblings about his performance lately, lack of attention to details, that type of thing. I'd hate to see something sidetrack such a promising career."

A quick flash of trepidation crossed Lyle's face that he quickly covered with a look of surprise. "Really? I haven't heard anything of that type and I'm right next door. I can't imagine who would be saying such things. Where would the FBI have been hearing such rumors?"

"It's probably nothing, just idle gossip—some second-hand information that apparently became garbled in the telling."

Lyle glanced at his watch. "It's almost noon. Are you available for lunch?"

"As it happens, I am. I have a field interview to conduct, but that's not until two o'clock. This will give us a chance to catch up. It's been six months since I was at your house for dinner. How are Margie and your two boys? If memory serves, the oldest one should be graduating high school next month."

"Yes, and he's been accepted to Harvard. It's going to cost a fortune, but it will be worth it when he gets that diploma."

The conversation at lunch settled on past cases they had been involved in, family matters and the current depiction of law enforcement in the movies and on television. They parted company at the entrance to the courthouse with Joe heading for his car and Lyle returning to his office.

An uneasy feeling settled in the pit of Lyle's stomach. It had been a strange meeting. Despite Joe's friendliness, there hadn't been any apparent reason for Joe Hodges's stopping by his office other than to try and solicit information about Frank James. He tried to dismiss it from his mind and returned his attention to the business of the day. He was prosecuting a case and needed to be in court first thing in the morning.

IT WAS LATE AFTERNOON WHEN Frank grabbed the phone and hit the speed-dial button. A moment later the man he answered to was on the phone. "I finally broke through the impressive array of obstacles on that car license plate from night before last. You're not going to like this. The car is registered to none other than Reece Covington."

The shock surrounded his words. "Reece Covington? Damn! That spells big trouble. How the hell did Brandi Doyle ever hook up with Reece? Are you aware of any existing connection between them before he went to prison?"

"I can't find anything that says she knew him even casually. I was finally able to take him down using Cindy Thatcher's talents, but he's much too shrewd for it to happen again. And this time he'll want his revenge. He'll be out for blood." There was now no doubt in Frank's mind that the man he had fought with inside Brandi's house was Reece Covington, and the slight twinge in his arm told him Reece had already drawn the first blood of revenge.

"Do you think he knows that you're involved?"

Frank took a steadying breath. He knew he had gotten himself into a bad spot. His boss was already unhappy with him. Did he dare admit to the personal encounter with Reece? He knew the answer to that one.

"I don't know how he could. Brandi didn't see me, so there's no way for Reece to know."

"Were you able to run down where he's living? That might be where the Doyle woman is hiding."

"No. The vehicle is three years old. He bought it new before going to prison. He paid cash so there's no financial institution involved. The registration was hidden behind a wall of dummy corporations. It took some digging before I even came up with his name in connection to any of it. The vehicle had to be stored somewhere while he was gone, so I suppose it could be in someone else's possession now even though Reece is out of prison. It's possible that it wasn't even Reece behind the wheel."

"But not too likely?"

Frank chose to ignore the insinuation. "The addresses don't lead anywhere. I also did a check on utilities and property tax. Nothing shows up in his name or in the name of any of the corporations used on the vehicle. He's done a masterful job of covering his trail."

"Knowing Reece Covington, I would have been disappointed at anything less. One thing for sure, you'll need to be extra cautious. It's possible that he has already figured out that the pictures hold the key to what is causing the Doyle woman's troubles, but if he stumbles onto *why* they are important he'll dig in until he gets what he wants. He's tenacious in that regard. So you'd better be right about having gotten all the negatives and prints."

Frank sat at his desk, the phone receiver still in his hand and the loud dial tone telling him the person he had been talking to had hung up—a person whose final words carried full authority along with an implied threat. A nervous anxiety churned in the pit of his stomach. Just how much trouble could Reece stir up?

Officially, Reece Covington was a private investigator who had lost his license when he was convicted of a crime and sent to prison for two years. Would anyone seriously take the word of a convicted felon over that of a decorated police lieutenant? And without the pictures, Reece didn't have any proof—even if he did have suspicions.

Frank drew in a deep breath, then slowly exhaled. He replaced the phone receiver in the cradle. He felt a little better. But was he only fooling himself?

REECE WOKE WITH A START that morning. The strangest dream had been playing through his mind for what seemed like hours, but he couldn't recall any of the details other than he knew it had to do with Brandi and the danger surrounding them. He quickly glanced around as if needing to get his bearings so that he could center himself in the day's reality. His bedroom door was closed. Brandi was most likely still asleep.

He grabbed a quick shower and dressed in a pair of

jeans and a sweatshirt. He headed for the kitchen and started the coffee before doing anything else.

As soon as the coffee was ready, he poured himself a mug and carried it out to the front porch. It had been nearly three o'clock that morning when they had finally called it a night and retired to their respective sleeping arrangements.

Sleep had not come easily for Reece. There had been too many things running through his mind, not the least of which was how much he would rather have been in his own bed with Brandi. That was a thought he knew he didn't dare dwell on. There were far more important items on the day's agenda…a day that was already off to a late start.

He had to discover exactly what it was that Frank James was after, and how Brandi had ended up on his bad side. And Reece needed to thwart Frank's attempts to get at her. Reece also had to expose Frank James for what he was, along with identifying Frank's colleagues and whomever it was that he reported to. It was a tall order.

Reece continued to turn the possibilities over in his mind as he sipped his coffee. Who were the most likely candidates to be the person Frank reported to? The big shot of his criminal operation?

"Good morning." Brandi's voice cut into his thoughts.

He turned as she stepped out onto the porch. "I see you found the coffee."

"Yes." She took a sip from her mug. "The aroma sent me straight to the kitchen."

"I suppose we'd better get something to eat, then settle down to business."

They compromised on brunch rather than breakfast or lunch. After they ate, he checked his e-mail. He got the information from Brandi so he could pull up her e-mail, too. He called to her.

"Take a look at these. Two of them have attachments."

She leaned over his shoulder and read the information on the computer screen. She pointed to the second one. "That one is from my agent."

He opened the e-mail, printed it off, then downloaded the attached zip file. It contained a dozen photographs. He put all twelve of them up on the screen as thumbnail images. He turned toward Brandi, who stood behind him.

"Are these your photographs? The ones you sent to your agent? She sent twelve pictures as a zip file attachment to her e-mail. Is that how many pictures you sent to her?"

"According to the file copy of the cover letter I sent along with the photos, I referenced twelve identification numbers from negatives. That should be all of them." She squinted at the small images. "As I said, just beauty shots…pretty scenery. I tried to capture light and shadow contrast, interesting juxtaposition, striking weather patterns. I can't imagine what could be there that would be some kind of a threat to anyone or warrant someone coming after me and stealing my pictures. They're the same type of pictures that anyone else could have taken. The locations weren't difficult to get to. It wasn't like I had to hike through miles of wilderness to find that specific spot. I came across them while driving down various back roads, but nothing so rugged that an ordinary car couldn't navigate it with ease."

"I'm going to print out a hard copy of each picture, then we'll check every one on screen by zooming in on each grid section of the image. If we see anything that seems out of the ordinary, we'll crop that specific section and print it."

He worked for the next several hours, first printing out each picture in the largest size possible for his printer and the best quality available, then slowly and meticulously going over each photograph on the computer monitor, inch by inch. It was the eleventh photograph before he spotted anything out of the ordinary.

"What's this? It looks like some people in the background of the shot." He turned to face her. "Are you aware that you took a picture with people in the background?"

"Yes, but they were so far away that they weren't recognizable. I thought they brought some interesting definition to the scene, an added dynamic. There's this beautiful water setting, serene and peaceful and seemingly out in the middle of nowhere, with four unidentified people enjoying the afternoon at the lake and the wonders of nature. A moment of man and nature coming together in harmony."

He cocked his head and shot her a quizzical look. "*Four* people? There are only three people in this photograph." He quickly clicked on the next picture, the last one of the twelve and the same locale, and zoomed in on the same area of the background. "There are only three people in the background of this picture, too." He turned to her. "Are you sure there were four people present?"

"Yes, I'm sure. My first thought was two couples, possibly on a picnic. Then I realized that it was three men and one woman. I wasn't close enough to really see what they looked like, and since I wasn't using a telephoto lens I knew they wouldn't be recognizable in the photograph, either."

She wrinkled her brow in a moment of confusion. "Are you sure you don't see four people? There wasn't a car, at least not that I could see, so I don't know where the fourth person could have gone."

"Let me give this a closer look. Maybe one of the trees is obscuring the view of the fourth person. Right now I've zoomed in as far as I can on that section and still have a viable image," Reece explained. "I'll try to enhance and fix the pictures so that the faces of the people are recognizable, but I don't know how much I'll be able to manipulate them on this computer with this software. We might need to have your agent rescan them using a much higher resolution, so we can blow them up larger and still retain the sharp definition we need in order to see an identifiable face."

"Do you want me to call her now?"

He turned the thought over in his mind. "Yes. I think only these two pictures with the people in the background need to be rescanned immediately. I'd like for her to do all of them, but if she can do these two right now and send them immediately it will be very helpful.

If possible, it would be great if she could do the rest of them tonight and send them in the morning. Here—" he jotted some numbers and letters on a piece of paper "—these are her file names on the two pictures I want rescanned."

Brandi made the phone call while Reece continued to work with the images. He worked with the two photographs for almost an hour before shoving back from his desk. He shook his head in frustration.

"We need those rescanned images. There just isn't enough detail here to work with. I can't bring the people in clear enough to be recognizable."

Brandi glanced at her watch. "My agent said she could rescan the two photographs and send them by seven o'clock tonight. They should be here pretty soon."

The ringing sound interrupted their conversation. He grabbed the cell phone from the desk, checked the caller I.D., but didn't recognize the number. It was finally the fourth ring before he decided to answer it.

"Yes?"

"Reece? It's Joe. Did I catch you at a bad time?"

"No…not at all. Did you come up with anything on Frank?"

"Sorry. I've checked our files and made a couple of discreet inquiries of friends in other federal agencies and there just isn't anything. I kept getting the same answer. No one ever heard of Frank James. He's an unknown person in federal circles except for a couple of people assigned to the local Seattle office."

"Are you sure? Nothing at all? Not even a whisper?"

"As I mentioned when we had lunch, I've only met

him once in passing so I don't have any firsthand knowledge about him. I could ask a few more questions if you'd like, but I don't think I'm going to come up with anything different. He's apparently just another local cop with nothing special to set him apart from any other. Sorry I couldn't find anything specific for you. What does this do to your friend's problem?"

"I'm not sure." Reece quickly finished the call, not wanting to stay connected any longer than absolutely necessary.

He pulled Brandi into his arms. "That was Joe Hodges. He claims no one in federal circles even knows Frank, let alone having any information about him floating around."

"Do you believe him?"

"I'm not sure, but I'm glad I decided not to mention your name or give him any specifics about what's been happening." He tried to shake away the sense of foreboding that jittered through his body. Had he made a big miscalculation in contacting Joe? Had he been away from the game long enough that he had lost his edge? One thing he did know for sure, he couldn't afford any more slipups. Brandi's life was at stake.

"Why didn't you tell him about the bullet and the shell casing? Weren't you planning to send them to him to check against unsolved crimes using that type of gun?"

"Yes, that was my intention. But I think I'd like to give it a little more thought before I do anything. I've got an uneasy twinge gnawing at me and I'm not sure what it means."

He checked Brandi's e-mail. A feeling of relief washed over him when he saw that the rescanned pictures were there. He downloaded them. This time he knew exactly what he was looking for. He zoomed in on the section of the first picture that contained the people. He cropped that area, then printed just the grouping of the people as a full-page print. Then he did the same thing to the second picture. He picked up the large print of the cropped section of the first photograph. He grabbed a magnifying glass and studied the enlarged image of the people under the direct light from his desk lamp.

His breath froze in his lungs and his voice died in his throat. He dropped the photograph on the desk and set the magnifying glass next to it. It was a moment before he could force out the words. "I don't believe it."

"What did you see?"

He handed the photograph and magnifying glass to Brandi. "Take a look. See anyone you recognize?"

She took the photograph and magnifying glass, held the picture under the lamp to catch the maximum amount of light and looked through the magnifying glass. She studied the faces of two of the men in the photograph. The third man had his back to the camera. "Isn't that Frank James?"

Reece took the picture and magnifying glass from her. "That's exactly who it is."

"I don't understand. What would be so critical about a police lieutenant being photographed in a mountain setting?"

"That in itself is unimportant, as you said. It's the other man who makes the difference."

"Who is he? I don't recognize him."

"His name is Mitch Mantee. He's one of the top organized crime figures on the West Coast."

Her eyes grew wide as the full implication registered in her mind. She took another close look at the photograph. It was clear that the crime boss was handing an envelope to Frank James.

"It looks like a payoff." She locked eye contact with Reece. Her heart pounded in her chest, and a hint of panic tried to work its way into her voice. "I took a photograph of an organized crime figure making a payoff to a police lieutenant?"

"That's sure the way it looks. Retrieving these pictures, both negative and prints, was vital to them. They also needed to know whether you were aware of them being in the shot, if you recognized who they were, had you made other copies of the pictures that you sent to anyone or had you told anyone about what you caught on film. Not having the answers to those questions is probably the only thing that kept you alive."

Reece inspected the second picture. After the shock of the first grouping of people in the background, the next one was the icing on the cake. "I'll be damned!"

"What's wrong?" Brandi stared over his shoulder at the photograph. "What do you see?"

"It's your fourth person, the woman. This picture is Frank James, Mitch Mantee and Cindy Thatcher. The other man must have been blocked from the camera's view by the tree."

"Who's Cindy Thatcher?"

He took in a steadying breath. His past seemed to

have come full circle to confront him. "She's a woman who hired me to find her missing brother. I found him, but it turned out that he wasn't her brother at all. He was a man who had gone into hiding in fear of his life because of his dealing with some shady characters. I never did know those details. He ended up dead. It all turned out to be a setup that resulted in my arrest and two years in prison."

"Who was the man?"

"Now that I'm seeing these pictures, I'd say that he was someone the mob wanted to find and hadn't been able to. Not even Frank, with the facilities of the police department at his beck and call, had been able to locate him since he had gone into hiding on his own rather than being in police protective custody. So, they had Cindy hire me and they used me as their bird dog. It served two purposes—they found the man they had been looking for, *and* Frank James was able to finally get me out of the way. He had tried without success on a couple of occasions to get my P.I. license revoked. By framing me and lying on the witness stand so that I ended up convicted and in prison, he finally got it done."

Reece looked at the picture again. "So here it is, all wrapped up in a neat and tidy package. The woman who set me up, with the cop who arrested me and perjured himself on the witness stand, in a secluded setting taking a payoff from a high level organized crime figure. Brandi, you have more here than merely a couple of photographs of beautiful scenery with some unidentified people in the background."

He made eye contact with her. "You've captured

dynamite on film, incriminating evidence that could put all the participants in prison. I only wish we could see the face of the third man."

But it was even more than that. It also told Reece that Frank was desperate and would stop at nothing to make sure his secret dealing remained just that—a secret.

Brandi was in even more danger than he originally realized. And now so was he.

Every move they made, every decision about what path to follow, had to be carefully thought out. They couldn't afford any mistakes. One little misstep could spell disaster.

He knew he needed to talk to Joe Hodges again. There was no way of getting around it. But now he needed to rethink what he would say to the FBI agent and exactly how much of the truth he would reveal.

Should he casually drop Mitch Mantee's name in conversation and wait for a reaction from Joe? And then there was the cartridge and casing from Frank's pistol. He felt sure that there would probably be at least one unsolved crime connected to the ballistics, possibly more.

The question was whether Joe could be trusted with all the details. Lives were at stake, both Brandi's and his. Where would Joe's priorities lead him? To protect the innocent or get Mitch Mantee regardless of the consequences? It could even be possible that if Joe knew exactly what was going on he might try to use Brandi as bait to lure Mitch into the open. It was not the type of behavior he would have associated with Joe in the past, but Reece had a personal stake in this...a very personal stake. He couldn't afford to overlook any possibilities. It was a troubling situation.

Chapter Eight

What had been a confusing problem had now become a major disaster for both Brandi and Reece. There were two unanswered questions that still nagged at him, questions that needed answers.

Who was the third man in the picture with his back to the camera? Was it one of Mitch Mantee's men, possibly his bodyguard? Or was it someone who worked with Frank James? The person Frank James reported to? Maybe even someone in a trusted position of authority with either the police department or possibly some other governmental office.

And of even more concern was the other unanswered question. Did Mitch Mantee know what had happened, or was Frank trying to contain the situation on his own? Hopefully Frank had the good sense to keep the problem to himself and to try to handle it without any outside help from organized crime. But good sense wasn't always one of Frank James's long suits. He was smart, but sometimes he acted impulsively without giving it rational thought.

The anxiety churned inside Reece. Having a known

person after them was one thing, but at least he knew who he was up against. If they had an unknown professional hit man on their trail it would be quite another problem. He glanced toward Brandi. Did she fully understand the implications? The expression on her face told him that she understood exactly what it meant and what was at stake.

Brandi wrapped her arms around his waist. "You don't need to say it. What was originally a stalker now turns out to be a larger problem—a *much* larger and even more deadly problem." She looked up at him. "And now I've put you in a position where you're in just as much danger as I am. I'm so sorry. If I'd had any idea...well, I could have gone to the FBI with the pictures and you wouldn't be in this danger and I could have gotten protection from them. Now...well, I just don't know..."

The words died in her throat. All she could think of was that she had been responsible for the danger that now threatened Reece, too. If anything happened to him, it would be her fault.

He tangled his fingers in the silky strands of her hair as he cradled her head against his shoulder. "That's not the way it is. First, you've given me the opportunity to confront the details of what happened to me. Now I have the opportunity to put that right. And second—" he brushed a tender kiss across her forehead "—if this hadn't happened I would never have met you. Something very special would have been missing from my life. I would always have had an empty place inside me that I would have been trying to fill without ever knowing exactly what I was looking for." The words had come from his heart even though it was more than he had anticipated saying.

More than he had wanted to admit.

He had a bad track record with relationships, starting several years ago when he had been left at the altar by his fiancée, who had decided to return to a former lover. And, of course, there was the disaster with Cindy Thatcher. For him to make yet another attempt at having a relationship, of making another commitment, had not been part of his agenda.

He continued to hold Brandi. He reveled in the closeness, yet his mind remained in turmoil over what to do about his relationship with her. The word *relationship* had become a little easier for him to acknowledge, but the overall meaning and the implied commitment still frightened him. As she'd said, everything had happened so quickly. Perhaps much too quickly. And then there was the fact that he didn't have any idea how she felt or what she wanted beyond the obvious of stopping the menace that haunted them.

Another thought put a stop to the direction his mind had wandered. Yes, things had come about very quickly. However, with the uncertainty that continued to surround them—the danger that seemed to be turning more perilous with each new discovery—time had become a precious commodity. If their time together could end up being much too short, then they should make the most of it.

Brandi looked up at Reece, a quizzical expression on her face. "Since you've identified an organized crime figure as being involved in this, doesn't that mean that federal authorities can do something? Wouldn't that fall under the FBI's jurisdiction?"

He pulled in a steadying breath, not sure of how to respond to her question. "Yes, technically that makes it federal jurisdiction."

"Can you call your friend, Joe Hodges, again? If you tell him about the pictures and the crime boss, won't he step in and take care of things? Bring in other agents and put an end to Frank James and his network?"

An uneasy feeling continued to ripple through his body. His last conversation with Joe had left him uncomfortable, even though he still didn't know exactly why. He would call, but he also had every intention of proceeding cautiously, and *no* intention of mentioning Brandi's name even if Joe demanded to know all the facts.

He paused for a moment, trying to gather his thoughts in some sort of logical order. "Yes, I'm going to call Joe again, but first I need to figure out exactly what to say to him. I'm not sure how to approach the subject of the pictures, or the spent cartridge and shell casing from Frank's pistol. I don't want to just blithely hand everything over to Joe and find out that we've been lost in the shuffle, that we've been hung out to dry and left to fend for ourselves. On the other hand, this has become big enough that it's not realistic to think that we can handle it alone to the point where we can turn over everything in a neat package with all the loose ends tied up."

She closed her eyes and rested her head against his

shoulder. A little shudder of despair rippled through her body. "I'm so sorry. I never should have involved you in my problems."

"It's as much my problem because it involves my past as it is your problem in the present. That makes it *our* problem. We'll handle this together. We just need to figure out the best way of handling it."

He flashed a confident smile. "Everything is going to be okay."

Something about Reece Covington made her feel as if his words were more than merely empty rhetoric, that everything truly would work out just as he had said. Everything about him exuded confidence and security, the type of strength that told her he could handle whatever type of situation came his way. As long as he was in her life, nothing bad could happen to her. But how long would he be there?

Reece's voice interrupted her troubled thoughts. "I think it would be a good idea if I e-mailed a copy of the pictures to my P.I. friend, and then mailed him a hard copy of the blown-up prints along with the second spent cartridge and shell casing from Frank's pistol. I'll tell him to keep them in a secure place as an added precaution in case someone manages to track the pictures as far as his computer. That will prevent anyone from hacking into his computer and destroying the pictures with a virus in hopes of eliminating our evidence. It's like having a double backup system. We have our evidence locked in the floor safe, Joe will have the pictures and ballistics evidence, and my friend will have both the pictures in his computer and the pictures and ballistics evidence in a secure location in another state."

His desire, his need for the closeness finally won out over his attempt to keep the conversation going. He rested his cheek against the top of her head and took a steadying breath.

"Brandi…I don't want to assume more than I have a right to, but I've got to be honest with you." He felt her body stiffen. Did he dare continue? He forced out the words, knowing that he had to finish what he had started to say.

"I don't know about you, but I've been experiencing a growing closeness between us…something that started out as a physical attraction that has become something more. I know these circumstances are a long way from ideal, and it's true that we haven't known each other very long, but I want to make love to you. What I don't want is for you to feel like you're being pressured into something you don't want, that the circumstances make you feel that you can't say no."

He took a step back from her. "I don't like playing games. I don't like it when a woman pretends that she needs to be seduced rather than simply being honest. And I don't want to have to second-guess what your words really mean. Don't say no if you really mean yes because I'll accept your no to mean just that—no. And that will be the end of it."

She reached her mouth to his, brushing a tender kiss across his lips. He wrapped his arms around her again. A bit of hesitation rippled through his body. "Is that a yes?" He held his breath as he waited for her response.

"That's a yes." Had she totally lost all reason and sanity or was she being as honest with herself about what she wanted as he had been with her? An honesty she had never faced before—with a man she couldn't have resisted even if she'd wanted to.

She made eye contact with him. She saw the same honesty she had seen when she'd first encountered him. She wanted—no, she *needed*—the feeling of a shared closeness and intimacy, something that had been missing from her life for a long time. Something that would tell her she was not alone even if it was only for one night. She was fully aware that he had made no promises about the future, had not mentioned any type of a commitment.

Reece held her close to him. They had all night to share their passion. Hours in which to relish the closeness and intimacy he had not known in years and with a woman who was far more than just a ship passing in the night. A woman in trouble who sincerely needed his help. An enticing woman he wanted as part of his life, more than just a casual bed partner.

He brought his mouth down on hers, taking possession of her addictive taste. His tongue darted into the recesses of her mouth—exploring, tasting, teasing, demanding…and possessing.

Brandi welcomed his kiss, his touch—and the delicious ecstasy they promised. She didn't know how, but she knew everything would turn out all right. With his help, she would be able to put a stop to the nightmare that had invaded her life and see to it that her abductor was brought to justice. She closed her eyes and totally gave herself over to the primal need coursing through her body.

Reece swept her up in his arms and carried her into the bedroom, depositing her gently on the edge of the bed. He took a calming breath as he reached out and caressed her cheek with his fingertips. The creamy texture of her skin sent a ripple of anticipation through his body. It had been a long time since he had been with a woman, but even if it had only been yesterday he still would have been awed by her.

And he had to admit to himself that he was just a little worried about his ability to provide what she wanted and needed.

The flush of delight covering her face and the fervor in her eyes told him she was as aroused as he was. He kneeled down next to her, pulled her into his arms and captured her mouth with a demanding intensity. His tongue meshed with hers in a dance of seduction. The kiss deepened, their passions soared.

As if they had made love together before, each seemed to instinctively respond to the other's desires. Pieces of clothing fell away. They scooted up to the middle of the bed, bare skin touching bare skin as his torso stretched out next to her body. He cupped her breast in his hand. Her soft moan of delight fed his excitement. He teased her nipple with his tongue before drawing the tautly puckered bud into his mouth, then he gently suckled.

Brandi arched her back, forcing her breast tighter against his mouth. Waves of excitement flowed through her body. She skimmed her fingertips across his muscular back at the same time as she ran her foot along the edge of his calf. She wanted more of him—

much more. A shiver of delight accompanied the sensation of his hand gliding up her inner thigh.

She melted under his touch when he inserted his finger between her delicate feminine folds. She had never had a man's mere touch send so much ecstasy coursing through her body. It wasn't just the passion of his kiss, the sensuality of his caress or the surge of sexual desire elicited by his touch. There was the man himself—his concern, his strength, his intelligence and his compassion.

He grabbed a condom from the box in the nightstand drawer. They had been an impulse buy at the time he'd bought the socks, the jeans and the computer supplies—wishful thinking on his part that had turned into reality. A moment later he nudged her legs apart with his knee. He situated his body over hers. His hard arousal slowly penetrated into the moist heat of her body. He paused as the incredible sensation swept through him. He set a slow, even pace. She met every one of his down strokes with an equally enthusiastic upward thrust of her own.

The intensity increased as they moved in harmony until the ultimate rapture claimed them. The convulsions spread through her body as the hard spasms shuddered through his. They clung to each other, savoring the euphoria of their union.

He held her tightly, placing tender kisses on her cheeks and forehead. He smoothed her hair away from her damp face. Making love to Brandi had been far more than merely the satisfaction of the physical act. It hit him with a profound emotion that he had not anticipated. His life was in turmoil, his future uncertain. He had nothing to offer her.

Yet he knew he couldn't let her go.

He brushed a tender kiss across her lips. "Are you okay, Brandi? Is there anything I can get for you?"

"I'm fine. I don't need anything at all." Nothing other than knowing if there was a chance for them to have a true future together when the upheaval in their lives had been resolved. Did she dare hope he felt the same way? She snuggled into his arms, for the moment feeling safe and secure. Everything between them had all happened so quickly, yet it all felt so very right.

But what would the light of morning bring? Would he turn distant? Had she made a colossal error?

No. Regardless of what the future held she would never regret having made love with Reece Covington. If that was all there was, it would be a memory that would live with her forever.

IT WAS LATE THAT MORNING when Reece finally woke up. Brandi was still wrapped in his arms, just the way they had fallen asleep. He watched her for a few minutes, afraid to move and disturb her. They had spent the night sharing their passion and hadn't stopped until the early hours of the morning. No one and nothing had ever had the type of impact on him that making love to her did.

He also knew that it put something else at stake. What had started as a tentative alliance, an offer by him to help her with her stalker based primarily on the possibility that Frank James might be involved, had turned into so much more. He also knew it was something they had to hold in abeyance until they resolved the danger surrounding them.

Brandi stirred, drawing Reece away from his thoughts. Her sleep-filled voice belied the sparkle of delight glowing in the depths of her eyes. "Good morning."

He placed a tender kiss on her forehead. "Good morning to you, too. Did you sleep well?"

She stretched her legs and wiggled her toes. "Never better."

"Me, too." He held her close, enjoying the warmth of the moment. To be able to wake up every morning with her in his arms would truly make his life complete. If only it could be a reality. If only his life could be so settled and calm. And it wasn't just *his* life. Her life was in chaos, too. Life-threatening danger stalked her, a threat he had to prevent from destroying her.

He continued to hold her close. Neither of them spoke for several minutes. It was finally Brandi who broke the silence.

"As delightful as this is, we can't spend the day here." Yet there was nothing she would rather be doing. Being in Reece Covington's bed, safely cradled in the security of his strong arms, had brought her the first feelings of true calm she had experienced in a month. If only every morning could start just as that one had.

A reluctant sigh of resignation escaped his throat. "You're right. We need to get out of bed." But he made no effort to move. "Yep, we need to get up. We have work to do." He still made no effort to move.

She glanced at the clock. The shock jolted her into

an upright sitting position. "Look at the time! I had no idea it was so late. We really do need to get up."

He placed a tender kiss on her lips, then pulled back the blanket and slid out of bed. "Do you want to take a shower first? I'll make coffee." He leaned his face into hers and placed a kiss on her lips again. A sly grin tugged at the corners of his mouth. "Unless you'd like to share the shower with me."

She returned his teasing grin. "That sounds tempting, but it would probably lead to other things and we would most certainly end up not accomplishing what needs to be done."

He allowed an audible sigh of resignation. "I suppose you're right, although my suggestion sounds like more fun."

"It certainly does."

She watched as he left the bedroom headed for the kitchen. She grabbed some clothes and went to the bathroom. The shower spray felt refreshing, but it did not keep her thoughts from constantly straying to the night of heated passion they had shared—a magical night of lovemaking unlike any she had ever known. And equally prominent in her thoughts was what the future held. There was the immediate future, with the life-threatening danger lurking from Frank James. But there was also the ongoing future and what it would bring once Frank James and his associates were no longer a threat.

Would Reece Covington be part of that future? She refused to dwell on any emotional connection that might exist between them. There would be time to explore that possibility later—at least she hoped so.

She finished in the bathroom, dressed and went to the kitchen. She poured herself some coffee and fixed breakfast while Reece took a shower and dressed. They were soon ready for the day's business.

Reece placed a phone call to his friend in California. "Chip…I need a favor…a really big favor and it has to be in the strictest of confidence."

"Sure thing, Reece. What can I do for you?"

"I have some items I'm going to send to you, and I need for you to keep them in a bank safe deposit box. If anything happens to me, I need for you to get them into the hands of the FBI."

There was a moment of silence before Chip responded. "What the hell have you gotten yourself into? What's going on?"

"It's something so convoluted and strange that I wouldn't believe it myself if I wasn't in the middle of it. I can only tell you that if everything turns out the way it should, it will clear my record of the felony conviction and I'll have my P.I. license back." He glanced at Brandi, noting the worried expression on her face. "And there's more. There's an innocent woman whose life is at stake. I've got to do everything I can to see that she isn't harmed."

"Tell me what to do and you've got it."

"Thanks, Chip. I'm going to e-mail you a zip file with some pictures. Then as a backup precaution I'm going to ship you hard copies of the same pictures along with a sealed envelope containing some ballistic evidence. There will be a note inside the sealed envelope explaining what it is and where it came from. As I said, if anything happens to me I want you to take it all to the FBI."

"Okay. You've got my P.O. box number, don't you? That will keep it safe in case someone gets on to this and stakes out my house and office looking for the mail. I can take it directly from the security of my post office box to the bank and put it in the safe deposit box."

"Good. I'll e-mail the pictures in a few minutes and will ship out the package today express mail and mark it for next-day delivery. Thanks, Chip. I owe you one."

"Yeah…take care of yourself. Let me hear from you every couple of days so I'll know you're okay. And make it by phone rather than e-mail so I can hear your voice and know for a fact that it's you."

"You got it." Reece disconnected the call, then reached out and took Brandi's hand. Just the sensation of her skin against his sent a wave of calm through his body, replacing the nervous jitter that had been there.

She looked at him questioningly. "Now what?"

"Now we venture out to a post office that has no connection with this area, put the items in question into an express mailer and send them off to Chip. Then we call Joe Hodges again."

"Have you decided what you're going to say to Joe? How much you're going to tell him?"

"Not really, but I think it's important that I make contact with him again today. I'll let him take the conversation where he wants it to go—that way I can determine what's important to him so that I'll know how to proceed."

Reece turned on his computer and e-mailed the pictures to Chip. Next, he gathered up the other items that needed to go to the post office. When he was ready to leave, he turned toward Brandi and took her hand in his.

"I'm not sure what to do. On one hand I think you'll be safer staying here while I'm gone. Frank could have easily provided your picture to the local sheriff with a *report any sightings but do not approach* instruction. Even though he will have a difficult time tracing ownership of my vehicle, it's not impossible. He could also have added make, model and license plate number to the bulletin. But, on the outside chance that Frank may be on to something, I don't want to leave you here alone and unprotected like a sitting duck."

"I want to go with you. There has to be something I can do to help. I don't feel right about sitting safely out of the way while you risk your neck on my behalf. Besides, I'm accustomed to taking care of myself rather than letting someone else fight my battles for me."

The sound of a slow-moving truck grabbed their attention. He saw the moment of panic dart across her face, an expression that matched the surge of adrenaline pumping through his veins. He bolted for the cabin door, pulling Brandi along behind him. Once outside, he cautiously made his way around the corner of the cabin into the carport. He peered around the corner at the fire road, then breathed a sigh of relief when he spotted the forest service truck checking the road for storm damage.

He extended a bit of a sheepish smile. "I guess my nerves are a little on edge."

She swallowed the lump of anxiety that had lodged in her throat and tried to slow down her racing pulse.

"They had company. My nerves were sitting out on that ledge, too."

"Well, that settles the matter. You're coming with me. I don't want to subject you to a nerve-wracking experience every time a vehicle comes within earshot."

They gathered the items to take with them. At the last minute before stepping out the door, Reece turned toward Brandi and studied her for a moment. He grabbed a baseball cap and handed it to her.

"Here, wear this, Goldilocks. It will cover most of your hair so it won't be as obvious. That and some sunglasses will have to do for the time being."

He watched as she adjusted the size on the cap, put it on and tucked as much of her hair up out of sight as she could. They started for town again. He drove to Edmonds, a city about fifteen miles north of Seattle. After leaving the post office, they stopped at a grocery store for supplies. Then they returned to the cabin, arriving after dark. It had been a thankfully uneventful excursion as far as anything suspicious or alarming was concerned.

Reece began to feel a little more comfortable about their game of cat and mouse. He had protected their evidence in a manner that was beyond Frank James's grasp. Now he needed to set the other pieces of his plan into motion. It was time to call Joe Hodges again.

He dialed Joe's number. After four rings he connected to Joe's voice mail and left a message. On the chance that someone else might hear it, he did not identify himself, knowing that Joe would recognize his voice.

"I have some additional information for you, but you apparently aren't available. Don't bother calling me back. I'll call you when I have an opportunity." Then he disconnected the call.

Reece turned toward Brandi. "I don't want him to call the number I gave him at lunch the other day. Knowing Joe, he'll make the call after he's set up a cell tower trace. I want to keep control." A sly grin tugged at the corners of his mouth. "And then there's the added perk of making him wait to find out what else I have for him. I want to leave him slightly off balance so that he's scrambling to keep up with me rather than getting ahead of us."

Brandi tilted her head to the side and shot a quizzical look in his direction. "It sounds like you don't really trust him."

He pulled her into his embrace and held her for a moment before answering. "Right now I don't trust anyone. Obviously the introduction of Mitch Mantee has altered the situation, but I still want to maintain the maximum amount of control possible under the circumstances."

He continued to hold her, resting his cheek against her head. The stakes kept getting higher and higher. At first it was a woman in trouble. Then the added presence of Frank James upped the ante. And now everything was on the line with the involvement of an organized crime boss. He accepted the fact that they could no longer handle the situation by themselves, but that didn't mean he was willing to blindly trust someone else regardless of how long he had known that person. He would view Joe Hodges with caution.

"We need to get some sleep so we can get up at a decent hour in the morning and not have half the day gone before we get started. I want to call Joe first thing."

But sleep wasn't on his mind. He captured her mouth with a sensual kiss that clearly conveyed his intentions. Her immediate response signaled her agreement.

Chapter Nine

Reece and Brandi sat in his car in the shopping center parking lot in Bellevue, across Lake Washington from Seattle. He glanced at his watch—nine o'clock. He took a swallow of his morning coffee while waiting for Joe to answer his cell phone. He kept a watchful eye on the people going in and out of the grocery store. A moment later the familiar voice came on the line.

"Hodges."

"Good morning, Joe."

"Your message said something about additional information. What's up?"

He was pleased with the way Joe went straight to the business at hand without attempting any casual conversation. "I'll be brief since I'm sure you're busy and I know I am. I have a spent cartridge and its shell casing from a .25-caliber Beretta Bobcat. I'd like you to check it against any unsolved cases."

There was a moment's hesitation. "Whose pistol is it?"

Reece's voice took on a rigid attitude. "Not a valid question at this time. Ask me again when you have a match to an unsolved case."

"Okay...how do I get them?"

"I'll hand them over to you in one hour at the coffee bar inside the grocery store at the shopping center where Interstate 90 and 405 cross in Bellevue. I also have a little tidbit that might provide some incentive for you to help me with this."

"And what would that be?"

"Does the name Mitch Mantee ring any bells? I'll see you in an hour."

"Wait a minute! Don't hang up! Mitch Mantee? What do you know about him?"

"Not now, Joe. I'll see you in an hour."

"I'm not sure I can get there in an hour."

"Sure you can—requisition one of those shiny FBI helicopters that you have sitting around." Reece quickly disconnected the call.

A pleased grin spread across his face as he took hold of Brandi's hand. "The mention of Mitch Mantee should guarantee his presence...and on time, too."

"Why did you say in an hour?" She gestured out the window. "We're in front of the grocery store right now. Is he so far away that it will take him an hour to get here? A helicopter would mean that he could be here in a matter of minutes."

"Yes, but I want to make sure that Joe doesn't send someone ahead to stake out the place so they can follow me. We can observe everything that goes on between now and Joe's arrival. It will give me an opportunity to spot his men so we'll know who to keep an eye on."

"Will you tell Joe about me? I mean, tell him who your *friend* is? Will I be going inside with you to meet Joe?"

He wrinkled his forehead into a slight frown. "I haven't decided yet. It will depend on what happens between now and then. Keep your eyes open for the basic, nondescript four-door sedan with one or two men inside...anyone who looks like they're not here to make a purchase. Pay particular attention to the people hanging around at the gardening center by the front entrance to the grocery store, anyone who seems to be paying more attention to the people going in and out than to the items available for sale. And we're not necessarily looking for a man alone or two men. It could be a man and woman posing as a married couple, but still watching the other people rather than the plants and flowers."

A slight chuckle escaped her throat, part amusement and part nervousness. "You sound like you've been through this before."

"Just a few of the things I learned from Joe."

She tried to maintain an upbeat sound to her voice. "Is it always this stressful? It feels like my nerves are being stretched to the breaking point."

He leaned over and placed a tender kiss on her lips. Emotion filled his words. "I'm sorry to have to put you through this. My first choice was to leave you back at the cabin where you would be safer than you are here, but there's a good chance that I might need your help before we get out of here."

"Whatever you need for me to do, just let me know. As I said earlier, I don't want to sit around doing nothing while you're out risking your life on my behalf. This is my mess and I want to contribute to solving it."

He saw the apprehension in her eyes, but had to admit that she did an admirable job of keeping it out of her voice. "I've been turning everything over in my mind, and I think we should play out the meeting this way. After I see Joe go inside the grocery store, I'll join him. You stay in the car for a minute or so and keep your eye on the store entrance. Watch for anyone who's been hanging around, then follows me inside. You wait and enter the grocery store a couple of minutes later. Don't wait too long because I don't intend to be here more than just a few minutes. Take a seat close enough to me where we can make eye contact, and you'll hopefully be able to hear us as we talk. When I give you a nod, come back here and pull the car around to the front entrance. Scoot over to the passenger seat and leave the engine running. I want to be able to jump into the driver's seat and get the hell out of the parking lot before they can get to their cars. Do you think you'll be able to do that?"

She extended a confident smile. "No problem." If only she felt as assured as the image she tried to project. She couldn't think of anything he had overlooked, but that didn't make her feel any easier about it. She knew that she had to share in the risk. She *wanted* to share in the risk. After all, it was her fault that he was in danger. She had full confidence in Reece Covington and his abilities. She glanced at him. She saw the tension etched into his handsome features as he scanned the parking lot, looking for anything that seemed out of place.

Her mind drifted to the previous night when they had made love. Not only had he fulfilled her physical needs, he had fulfilled her emotionally as well. She desperately wanted to plan for the future, to think beyond the here and now, but she knew there was no future as long as the danger continued to stalk them.

They remained in his SUV, keeping a watchful eye on the people coming and going while talking quietly about other things. He purposely tried to keep the conversation focused on topics having nothing to do with the circumstances of the moment. He wanted desperately to ease her mind, to help break the tension and relieve the stress he knew had to be churning her insides into knots. He also wanted to talk about the future, about their lives after this nightmare was resolved and the danger surrounding them no longer existed. He wasn't exactly sure what he wanted for the future, but he knew what he did not want—he did not want to lose her from his life.

But it was a topic that would have to wait until another time.

Reece jerked to attention. "There." He pointed toward the entrance of the store. "See that man in the blue windbreaker and gray slacks? The one with his hand to his ear carrying the newspaper?"

"Yes. Who is he?"

"*Who* he is, I don't know. But I'll bet my last dollar that I know *what* he is. He has FBI written all over him. Make sure you keep him in sight. He might stay outside while I'm inside or he might follow me into the store. If he follows me inside, then you can bet there's at least one more agent who will be outside." He glanced at his watch. "Our meeting isn't scheduled for half an hour yet. Joe certainly got his forces mobilized in record time. He always did get high marks for efficiency."

Brandi studied the people around the store entrance. "Do you see any more people who might be FBI?" She zeroed her gaze in on another man at the gardening center. "What about that one in the light blue ball cap? He's not dressed for gardening. If he buys anything, he'll need to change clothes before he can do anything with it once he gets home."

Reece flashed a pleased grin at her. "Good catch. The time frame didn't allow for Joe to muster any available undercover agents who would more easily blend in. He had to pull from agents on duty and get them here immediately."

He glanced at his watch again. "Joe should be arriving any minute. Or, more accurately, making his appearance from wherever he's been hiding."

He clenched his jaw into a hard line of determination. He had been mentally sorting through several thoughts and had come up with a new scenario. "I'm changing the plan." He saw the immediate surprise that covered her face. "I have an idea that I think will work more to our advantage."

She looked around, then returned her attention to him. "Did you see something? Why have you decided to change things?"

He started the car and drove toward the entrance of the grocery store, stopping about thirty feet from the front entrance. He sat behind the wheel with the engine idling as he scanned the area looking for Joe Hodges.

"I'm taking Joe for a ride with us rather than talking

to him here. It will be pretty easy to determine if someone is following us and will put us in control of the situation without his men standing by. The only downside is that it will allow him to see you even though I won't be telling him who you are. Is that going to be okay with you?"

She wrinkled her brow into a momentary frown. "I'll do whatever you think is best."

He continued to watch the grocery store entrance while scanning the area until he spotted Joe. "There he is…fifty-nine minutes from the time I told him to be here in one hour. Sometimes Joe can be very predictable, but every now and then he has surprised me by doing something totally unexpected. So far, today isn't one of those surprising times. Let's hope it stays that way."

Reece leaned over to Brandi and placed a tender kiss on her lips. "It's show time." He saw the apprehension in the depths of her eyes. He extended a confident smile. "Everything will be okay."

He took a calming breath to steady his nerves, then put the car in gear and eased the vehicle forward, coming up behind Joe. A low-level anxiety churned inside him. He wasn't completely happy with the plan he had devised, but he didn't know what else to do. Things would have been so much easier if Joe hadn't left him with such an uneasy feeling. He'd much rather have had Joe as an ally instead of a possible adversary. But it was too late now. The wheels were in motion, and all he could do was make the best of what he had to work with.

He pulled alongside Joe, stopped and rolled down his

window. "Nice of you to come out on this sunny morning. Climb into the backseat and we'll go for a ride." He saw the surprise on Joe's face, but the FBI agent did as he was told without hesitation. Before Joe even had his door closed, Reece sped out of the parking lot. He made a few quick maneuvers around corners, through parking lots and down alleys before finally entering the interstate and heading toward downtown Seattle.

When he finally felt confident that they weren't being followed, he turned his attention to Joe. "I'm disappointed in you, Joe. I saw a couple of your men at the store. The first one on the scene arrived about half an hour before you did. My intention was to have a private conversation with you, not hold court in front of several FBI agents. You make me feel like a criminal rather than one of the good guys."

Joe leaned back in the seat, attempting to project a casual manner. "I've got to hand it to you, Reece. Being in prison didn't dull your edge or your instincts." He glanced in Brandi's direction. "I don't believe I've met your friend."

"Don't tell me that you've forgotten Trixie DeBoop…the woman I was living with before I was framed and sent to prison?" Reece glanced at Brandi. "Trixie, this is Joe Hodges. He's with the FBI."

A hint of sarcasm surrounded Joe's words. "A simple *it's none of your business* would have sufficed."

Joe shifted his position in the backseat, moving to the other side of the car behind Brandi where he had a better sideways view of Reece. "If you're satisfied that we're not being followed, could we get down to business? I've got two questions—where is the cartridge and the shell casing you want me to check, and of even more importance, what does this have to do with Mitch Mantee?"

"Trixie, honey…hand Joe that envelope using the tissue so you don't leave any pesky fingerprints on it."

Brandi did as Reece had instructed. Joe took it from her, then read the information Reece had written on the envelope, stating the date and time of the test firing along with the make, model and serial number of the pistol.

"Where did the pistol come from? Who owns it, and how did it come to be in your possession?"

"When you run a check on the serial number you'll probably find that it was stolen—possibly a factory shipment of new pistols en route to a retailer, which would make the serial number a cold trail. As to how it came to be in my possession…I took it away from a man who intended to do me harm."

"And who would that be? You seem to have a great deal of interest in Frank James. Would he be the person wielding the pistol in question?"

"Don't push me."

"You're certainly being cagey with your answers this morning."

"I've got to be honest with you, Joe. You didn't instill any feelings of confidence in me at lunch the other day. The farther I get into this mess, the more startling the information I uncover and the bigger it becomes. I need your help with this, but I don't intend to be your sacrificial lamb. I'm not interested in you putting my life at risk to get what you want. And worse yet, putting my friend's life at risk in the process."

Joe took another quick glance at Brandi, raising a questioning eyebrow. Then he returned his attention to Reece. "Understandable. I'll run this through the computer and see if I can come up with a ballistics match. I suppose you want to know what I find?"

"Of course."

"Now, what about Mitch Mantee?"

"I have a couple of very incriminating photographs of Mitch Mantee that I'm sure you'd find very interesting."

"Photographs?" Joe visibly jerked to attention, his expression saying Reece had hit a home run. "Let me see them."

"I'm sorry. I didn't mean to imply that I had them on me. I only meant that they're someplace safe and I can put my hands on them with a proper amount of notice."

"Then let's do it."

"One step at a time, Joe. One step at a time. First, let's see what your computer says about the ballistics information." Reece fixed Joe with a quick moment of eye contact. "And speaking of Frank James...have you done any more digging? Have you come up with anything on him?"

"Nothing more than I've already told you. I only met him once, and I haven't found anyone who really knows him. Sorry, but there's just nothing new to report."

After about ten minutes Reece dropped Joe off at a Pioneer Square restaurant in Seattle and quickly disappeared into the traffic. They started back to the cabin by a route that kept them away from Bellevue and the grocery store location where he had met Joe. Reece remained deep in concentration, not offering any conversation. Something continued to tug at his consciousness, some little thing that had happened—something that should have triggered a concern at the time. He searched his mind, going over every moment of the time Joe had been in the backseat. After about ten minutes, he abruptly pulled into a parking lot at an office building.

The startled expression covering Brandi's face matched her voice. "What's the matter?" She quickly glanced around, then returned her attention to Reece. "Why are we stopping? Is there something wrong?"

He slid out from behind the wheel, opened the back door and climbed into the backseat of the SUV where Joe had been sitting. "Something's been bothering me and I just figured out what it was. Why did Joe shift his position from one side of the car to the other?"

"I thought he wanted to sit where he could see your face rather than the back of your head."

"Yeah, that was my thought at the time. But now I'm not so sure. He agreed to everything too easily. He didn't offer even one word of objection to getting in the car and being driven away nor did he try to stall for time. I'm sure we weren't followed. In fact, there didn't appear to me to have been any attempt at following us even though he had men on the scene. That only leaves one possibility—he brought something into my car so his men could track us."

"Maybe you should have searched him."

"I thought about it, then rejected the idea. We need his help. I didn't want to push him too far."

Her sincere concern filled her voice. "But he might have pulled a gun on you...arrested you."

"I wasn't concerned about that. He doesn't know what's going on, but he is smart enough to know that arresting me isn't going to get him the answers he wants. Besides, he has no grounds to arrest me. I haven't done anything illegal, and I certainly haven't violated any federal laws."

Brandi's gaze swept across the parking lot and out to the street. As much as she tried, she couldn't keep the anxiety out of her voice. "Do you think they're watching us right now? Are we in danger? I know it's the FBI, but...well, that part you said about being a sacrificial lamb...is that true?"

He looked at her, at the apprehension that covered her beautiful face. He heard the quaver in her voice. His heart went out to her, to the stress she had to be experiencing, and it rested heavily on his conscience. He should have left her back at the cabin where she wouldn't have heard the conversation. Perhaps that would have been easier on her. Then he recalled her words about being involved rather than being left behind.

Besides, it was too late now.

He reached out and lightly touched her cheek. He tried to keep the emotion out of his voice, but didn't quite manage it. "I'm sorry to put you through this. It will all be over soon. I can feel it. Before long you'll be able to return to your life and pretty soon all of this will be only a distant memory."

"And will you be able to return to the life you had before going to prison? Will the nightmare be over for you, too?"

It was a valid question, but he didn't know how to answer it. He leaned forward and brushed a tender kiss across her lips, then forced his attention back to the matter at hand.

"My guess is that he left something in the vehicle, probably a cell phone with GPS tracking. The time frame I gave him didn't allow for any fancy maneuvers on his part. I've been watching for helicopters in case he had one following him, but I haven't seen or heard any. He didn't need to have any of his men follow us in a car. They were tracking our location in real time. I think he changed positions to the other side of the seat to remove himself from the location of whatever he left."

Brandi watched as Reece looked under the front seats to see if Joe had shoved anything underneath from behind. Then he looked on the floorboards under the seat where Joe had been sitting, then where he had repositioned himself. He came up empty. Next he ran his hand down between the seat cushions. Just when he was about to consider his search a failure, his fingers closed around the object. He withdrew the cell phone. A smile of satisfaction pulled at the corners of his mouth.

"Joe thought he was pulling a fast one, and he almost got away with it. All he needed to do was offer a little bit of a protest at going with us and I never would have thought to look for something he purposely left behind. I hope the Bureau doesn't go too hard on him for the loss of his cell phone."

He opened it up and removed the battery, then removed the GPS chip. He dropped the chip on the ground and crushed it under the heel of his boot. He tossed the disabled phone into the glove compartment of his SUV.

"Why are you taking the cell phone with you? Wouldn't it be safer if you tossed it in the trash?"

"No. I removed the GPS chip, which allows the phone to be used as a tracking device, but the cell phone does belong to an FBI agent. I don't want to take the chance of someone finding it and being able to retrieve information even if it's only a list of recent incoming and outgoing phone calls. I don't want Joe tracking me, but I certainly don't want to compromise anything that could be sensitive. My guess is that leaving his phone was a desperation move. It was that or nothing and he knew he had to track me. Unfortunately for Joe, this is where the trail ends."

They got back into the SUV and headed away from Seattle. Even though Reece felt a little more comfortable, he still continued to check to make sure they weren't being followed. Yes, he might have felt a little more comfortable, but not all that confident. There were still some pieces of the puzzle that they needed in order to complete the picture.

"I've got one more stop to make before we head back into the mountains. I called in an order that I need to pick up. I may be giving in to a bit of paranoia, but better to err on the side of caution."

He pulled into the parking lot of an electronics supply store. "You wait here. I'll be right back."

Brandi watched as Reece disappeared inside the building. An electronics store—what could he be picking up that he thought was necessary to their safety? What type of electronics did the store sell? There wasn't anything visible that said it was computers, televisions, CD players or any other type of entertainment electronics.

He returned a few minutes later carrying a large box and a sack. He put the box in the back of the SUV, then opened the sack. He took out the small battery-operated meter, turned it on and slowly walked around the vehicle. Then he sat in the back behind the driver's seat. A wry grin turned the edge of his lips. He reached under the seat and found the small bug attached to the underside. He held it up for Brandi to see.

"That Joe is a sneaky one. He left the cell phone for me to find, hoping that would stop any further search. But he also planted this tracking bug. When someone is looking for something, once they find it they normally stop looking. I found the cell phone, so the theory says I would stop looking for anything else."

He started to drop it on the ground, then quickly changed his mind. "No, if I destroy it then it will obviously stop transmitting. That will tell Joe I found it. But if it continues to transmit, then he'll continue to track it. So—" he looked around the parking lot "—the thing to do is let it lead him on a wild goose chase."

Reece walked over to a van making a delivery and attached the tracking bug under the back bumper. The van would be constantly on the road, making lots of stops in all sort of places. He returned to his own vehicle. He slid in behind the wheel and they were on their way back to the cabin.

Brandi waited to see if he would volunteer what else he had purchased, but when he hadn't mentioned it by the time they arrived at the cabin her curiosity got the best of her. She watched as he took the carton from the back of the SUV.

"What's in the box?"

"Special thermal imaging cameras. They're battery operated with closed-circuit transmission. Not only do they work during the day, they also work at night without any lights. They pick up on heat sources, such as car engines and body heat. They transmit an image of the shape of the heat source. You don't see a picture of the person as in being able to recognize or identify a face, but they transmit the shape of whatever it is that's giving off heat, such as the figure of a person. They won't tell us who is approaching, but they will certainly let us know that something is approaching and what shape it is. We'll be able to distinguish between a deer roaming through the woods, a car and a person. We'll be able to tell how many people are in the car. If the people are on foot, we'll be able to see where they are and which direction they're moving. If they're hiding behind a tree, we'll know that, too."

She held the cabin door open for him as he carried

the box inside. "That sounds pretty sophisticated. Is it some type of new technology?"

"New technology? Nope. It's been around for a while. Both the military and law enforcement use it regularly. It's the type of thing you would use for a specific application, and it seemed to me that this was one of those. As I said, I have the ownership of my vehicle and the cabin hidden behind a barrage of obstacles. In fact, if someone manages to get through the maze on my car ownership, that won't lead them to this cabin. But that's not to say that someone who is determined enough and has the resources at his disposal won't be able to ultimately find this place. So, this type of thermal imaging surveillance is yet another precaution. It will give us a warning that someone is approaching."

She collapsed into the large chair, the one she had occupied when Reece first saw her. She shook her head in dismay, her troubled expression saying as much as her words. "You make it sound so simple and straightforward, almost like a game of cops and robbers. But the truth is that I'm feeling more isolated and apprehensive with each passing hour. You seem to be so confident and in control. I really admire that. As for me, my insides are tied in knots and what isn't knotted is quivering so much that I'm surprised you can't see it. I wish I was a braver person."

He kneeled down next to the chair, clutching her hand in his. "I think you've exhibited extreme bravery, especially in such unfamiliar circumstances. Just making the attempt to escape from your abductor is a sign of how brave you are. And having actually succeeded... well, that speaks for itself."

Once again his heart went out to her. Had he been pushing her too hard? Had his zeal to bring down Frank James and clear his own record overshadowed what was more important—the fact that her life was in danger?

He pulled her into his arms. "I don't know, Brandi... maybe it would have been better if I'd called Joe to begin with. He could have given you official protection. It wouldn't have felt as if we were digging a hole that we might not be able to climb out of. You would have been safe rather than sitting here in a mountain cabin hoping that no one finds you."

She mustered as much of a confident smile as she could. "What? And miss all this excitement? At least now I'll have some interesting stories to pass on to my grandchildren someday."

Her smile faded. "And don't forget...until we were able to examine those photographs we didn't know why any of this was happening. It would have been the word of some apparently neurotic female with a vivid imagination and an ex-convict against that of a police lieutenant. Would an FBI agent have believed us? Even one you knew personally?"

He caressed her shoulders and stroked her hair. His words were a mere whisper. "I may have handled this entire mess badly, but I'll always be grateful that our paths crossed."

Once again she saw the honesty in the depths of his eyes and felt the warmth flow through her body. When this nightmare was over she had to do whatever she could to make sure they had a future together. She could not allow him to slip out of her life.

He brushed a loving kiss across her lips, then stood up. "It's going to take a while to get the cameras properly situated outside, everything installed and the monitoring set up in here. I need to get the cameras in place before it gets too dark to see what I'm doing."

"Do you need some help? I don't know much of anything about electronics beyond how to program my VCR and turn on my computer, but at least I can hand you things as you need them."

He held out his hand and helped her up from the chair. "Let's get to work. I want it done as quickly as possible just in case…"

He didn't finish his sentence. He didn't need to. He knew they were both thinking the same thing.

AS SOON AS REECE DROPPED Joe at the restaurant, Joe called to be picked up. They immediately returned to the FBI office and Joe checked on the progress they had made with the tracking.

"It didn't take him very long, Joe. We lost the GPS tracking on your cell phone about ten minutes after he dropped you off."

Joe Hodges looked up from his computer where he had started a search for any unsolved crimes involving the use of a .25-caliber Beretta Bobcat pistol. "I'm not surprised. I didn't think that would last very long. Was there anything significant about the location where he stopped?"

"Nothing that jumps out at me. It was a parking lot

at an office building." A hint of a sarcastic chuckle escaped the agent's throat. "I'm surprised he didn't pick another grocery store."

Joe shot his colleague a harsh look. His voice held a stern warning. "Don't for one moment underestimate Reece Covington. If you do, he'll end up making you look like a fool. Grocery stores are good choices. They're neutral locations that don't stand out. All types of people and cars, constant activity of coming and going, easy to blend in with the surroundings. Grocery stores and their parking lots are ideal locations for meetings. I suspect the office building was simply a matter of convenience. He wanted to search the car and that was the first place he found where he could pull off the street and do it."

"At least finding your cell phone seemed to satisfy him for the time being and he apparently stopped his search. The tracking bug is still in place and transmitting."

"Where did he go after he found the cell phone?"

"He stopped at an electronics supply store. From there he seems to have made several stops at a weird assortment of places."

Joe shoved back from his computer and rolled his chair over to where the other agent was studying the tracking map on his computer screen. "Weird? In what way?"

"There doesn't seem to be any rhyme or reason to his stops. Small businesses, private residences. It's almost as if he's driving around aimlessly and stopping on impulse."

Joe checked a list of the locations. He shook his head

in resignation as he grudgingly acknowledged Reece's clever maneuver. "As I said, don't underestimate him. He's done it again, grabbed the upper hand when we thought we had it. Two years in prison certainly didn't take the edge off his ability or his inherent knack for survival. You say he stopped at an electronics supply place? I'll bet he purchased a meter to sweep for any type of a transmitting device. He found the bug and rather than destroying it, he attached it to some kind of a delivery truck. Since it's still transmitting, we think it's still hidden in his car. He goes on his merry way and we track some poor delivery driver all over town."

"How come you're letting Covington call the shots? We could have taken him into custody on the spot."

"On what charge?"

"Well, we could bring him in to answer questions—"

"No good. Timing is too critical right now. If we had pushed him he would have dug in and we wouldn't have gotten a thing from him. However, I have to admit that I don't like the idea of a loose cannon running around, possibly interfering with what we're doing."

"Do you want to continue tracking the vehicle?"

"No. Have someone retrieve the bug from the vehicle without the driver knowing it. What I do want is a list of everything Reece purchased at that electronics supply store. That might give us a lead as to where he's hiding and what he has planned. It might even help identify the woman who was with him. My theory is that she's the friend he mentioned at our lunch meeting, the one who he claimed was being stalked and was then abducted by Frank James. And if that's a fact, then it deepens our puzzle. Why would Frank stalk and abduct this particular woman? And then the million-dollar question: what does an organized crime boss have to do with Frank stalking some unknown woman? How does Mitch Mantee fit in? So far, I can't make any sense of this."

"You don't have any idea who the woman is?"

"None whatsoever. I thought about trying to do a match with Washington state driver's license pictures to see if I could identify her, but that's going to be a daunting task. Caucasian female in her early thirties... there have to be thousands of them, and it's something I have to do personally since I'm the only one who saw her and can make the identification. And even at that, she was wearing a baseball cap and sunglasses. I don't even know what color her eyes were or what they looked like. It's not something easy like matching a photograph of her against driver's license pictures where the computer can run a comparison check."

Joe shook his head as he mumbled more to himself rather than addressing his comments to anyone in particular. "I wish to hell I knew exactly what it was that Reece stumbled across and what that woman has to do with it."

"Have you come up on any kind of a ballistics match on what Covington gave you?"

Joe returned to his computer screen and clicked the print button. "So far, two unsolved homicides involving that type of weapon. Both occurred in Rocky Shores even though neither victim lived nor worked there. That put the investigation in Frank's jurisdiction. I'll have to do a comparison to the specific cartridge and casing Reece gave me, but I'll bet it's a match."

Joe glanced at his watch. "I have a racquetball game with Frank at four o'clock. I still have a few hours yet."

Chapter Ten

"How goes the search?"

The voice startled Frank James. He quickly minimized the information on his computer screen so that it was no longer visible, then turned toward his office door. An immediate wave of relief washed over him when he saw who was standing in the doorway.

"I'm still coming up blank. I thought he had his vehicle well hidden, but finding my way through that maze was a piece of cake compared to how well he's hidden the ownership of any real estate."

Frank's visitor glanced back over his shoulder at the policemen in the squad room, then closed the office door so he could talk to Frank in private. "It's possible that he doesn't own any real estate. He might be renting something, maybe a room somewhere that includes utilities. Since you haven't turned up any bank accounts for him, it would have to be on a cash basis. That's going to make it extremely difficult to come up with something."

"Good point." Frank furrowed his brow in a moment of concentration. "I thought about his driver's license providing a current address, but he was only in prison for two years. I checked to make sure, but it only confirmed what I suspected. When he got out his license was still valid so he didn't need to apply for a new one. It shows his address as being his home on Mercer Island, but he sold that while he was out on bail waiting for his trial date, which gave him a nice chunk of money so that he doesn't need to worry about any income for a while. But without any known bank accounts, I don't know where the money is. I've checked cell phone records and Internet accounts and came up empty. Either his cell phone is hidden behind the same series of veils as any real estate, or he's using a series of disposable cell phones with a constantly changing phone number."

"Well, we both know that Reece is a clever man—very resourceful and resilient. Look what it took for you to finally get him out of your way. Not only did you have to set him up and frame him with false evidence, you had to commit perjury on the witness stand in order to get his P.I. license yanked and put him in prison. And even at that, he was only in for two years. He did the smart thing by insisting on doing his full sentence rather than accepting parole. He walked out the prison doors with no strings attached and disappeared into thin air."

"You know—" Frank leaned back in his chair "—we could use the same tactic in getting rid of him again and at the same time get rid of the Doyle woman. When we find him, I'm sure we'll also find her. He kills her and we get him. If we stage it at her house here in Rocky Shores, that will put it in my jurisdiction so I'll be able to manipulate the evidence and control the investigation. Just like last time."

"That's all well and good, but first you have to find him. And when you do, you'll have to figure out some way of getting him and the woman both into custody and transported to her house without anyone in the department knowing about it other than your tight circle of hand-picked men. That's going to take some critical timing."

"Yes, I know."

"But first, find him."

Frank watched as his visitor left the office. He checked his watch. He had a racquetball game with Joe Hodges in a couple of hours. There wasn't anything specific he could put his finger on, but the entire situation with Joe showing up made him uneasy. And then there was the problem of his arm. Even though it was only a flesh wound, it was still giving him twinges of pain. Would it be better to call off the racquetball game? Claim a work conflict? Or muddle through and see what kind of information he could pick up about Joe's true purpose for being there? Whatever he decided to do, he would have to do it very soon.

He rotated his arm, mimicking the motions he would use while playing racquetball. Nope, it wasn't going to work. He reached for his phone and dialed Joe's number. A moment later he had the FBI agent on the phone.

"Joe, it's Frank. About our racquetball game for this afternoon...I'm afraid I have to postpone it. The assistant D.A. wants to have a meeting about a case that's coming up for trial, and I'm one of the key witnesses so I have to be there."

"No problem. We all know that business comes first and when business is putting the bad guys away we can't let it slide in favor of personal matters. Maybe next time I'm in your neighborhood we can reschedule it."

"Sounds good."

Frank kept up with a few minutes of casual conversation before terminating the call. Even though he had made his decision and Joe seemed to accept the cancellation without any problem, the situation continued to leave him with an uneasy feeling. Something was wrong.

Or was it just a case of rattled nerves? He knew he was playing a dangerous game by not disclosing his struggle with Reece and losing his backup pistol. He had to make that right before anyone found out about it. It was the type of mistake that could cost him his life if it got to Mitch Mantee.

Frank returned his attention to his computer search for anything that might lead to Reece Covington. The more he searched, the higher his frustration level rose. Two years in prison and the loss of the P.I. license hadn't changed anything. Reece was still in his face and making things difficult for him. Somehow Reece Covington had to be stopped.

Permanently.

REECE AND BRANDI FINISHED the outside installation of the cameras and set up the monitoring on the dining room table. Reece added an alarm system to wake them when images triggered the monitoring during the night.

After satisfying himself that everything was in proper working order, he turned his attention to other matters. "I'm starving. How about you? We didn't have much of a breakfast and skipped lunch."

"Me, too. I'm definitely hungry."

He heard the upbeat tone in her voice, but knew it only masked the anxiety etched on her face. He pulled her into his arms, his voice dropping to a seductive whisper. "The dining table seems to be unavailable. How about an intimate little dinner for two in front of the fireplace?"

"Sounds terrific."

He brushed a tender kiss across her lips, then reluctantly let go of her. Nervous energy coiled inside him like a tightly wound spring. The sound of thunder announced the arrival of the storm that had been lingering just off shore for a couple of days. "I think we're in for another bout of rain."

"Will that ruin the cameras or interrupt the transmission back here for monitoring?"

"Not as long as it's just rain, but a big-time lightning display could play havoc with it. If the power goes out, I'll kick on the emergency generator. It will supply enough power to handle the monitoring equipment and also the refrigerator so the food doesn't spoil. Other than that, we'll be reduced to fireplace, candles and a couple of kerosene lanterns for light and a battery-operated radio for news."

"Sort of like camping, only with a roof and a comfortable bed."

A soft chuckle escaped his throat. "And don't forget

the real bathroom with hot and cold running water and a flush toilet."

They went to the kitchen and fixed a quick meal. After they ate, Reece went to the floor safe and took out his 9 mm pistol and the holster. Legally, he wasn't allowed to have it in his possession, but the unusual and dangerous circumstances dictated otherwise.

Reece saw her apprehension as Brandi stared at the pistol. "Do you have any experience with firearms?"

She wrinkled her brow for a moment as she pulled up the memories from long ago. A hint of a tender smile tugged at the corners of her mouth. "Well, yes and no. Many years ago my father and I would have the occasional father and daughter day, as he liked to call it. We would go out in the country for target practice. We'd shoot at paper targets and tin cans with a rifle and a revolver he owned. Once he took me trap shooting… you know, the clay disks and a shotgun. I wasn't any good at that. I didn't like the way the shotgun recoiled into my shoulder."

She shook away the memories from the past as she pointed toward Reece's 9 mm semiautomatic pistol. "But I've never even held one of those, let alone shot one."

His voice told her what she already knew. There was no mistaking the seriousness that covered his features. "Perhaps a quick lesson is in order."

"What about the other one, the pistol you took from Frank and put in the safe?"

"I don't want to use that unless it turns out to be a dire emergency. The package I mailed to Chip includes the location of the safe and its contents. I don't think anyone searching the cabin will find the safe. Chip can pass that information on to the FBI in case something—"

She closed her eyes and wrapped her arms tightly around his waist. He didn't need to finish the sentence. A moment later his arms folded around her. Once again she felt his strength and determination flow to her, touching her senses and soothing her nerves.

She finally managed to find her voice. "What happens next? What are we going to do now?"

"We're going to call Joe again. By now he's figured out that his tracking bug hasn't been tracking us. He's also had plenty of time to check the ballistics on the spent cartridge and shell casing against any unsolved crimes using that type of pistol. We'll see what he has to say, how honest he's going to be with me, then decide from there."

He searched the depth of her eyes. He knew they were treading in dangerous waters, and he had to be honest with her. "We might have come to the end of the line as far as keeping your identity a secret. Now that we know a notorious organized crime figure is involved in local payoffs to the police, we could be arrested for withholding information even though we aren't aware of any specific investigation being conducted by the FBI."

"I knew you wouldn't be able to hide me from the FBI for long, regardless of what you said to Joe in the car." She took a calming breath. "It's time for *Trixie* to come clean and confess the truth."

"I'll call Joe again. I'm sure he's anxiously waiting

to hear from me. In fact, I'm surprised he hasn't tried to call me with the results of the ballistics search." He allowed the frown to spread across his forehead. "In fact, it's odd that he hasn't tried to call me about that. Damn—I hope I didn't misread him. I figured the mention of Mitch Mantee would be enough to guarantee his cooperation."

He brushed a tender kiss across her lips. "I don't want to let Joe know where we've been hiding and who you are until he can guarantee that the FBI will give you protection, and he can't do that until he has a violation of federal law. He can't arbitrarily protect you against a local law enforcement officer based on nothing more than suspicion of wrongdoing without any proof."

"But won't the picture of Frank taking the payoff from a known organized crime boss be enough proof?"

"It's strong circumstantial evidence but without other evidence it won't be enough as there's nothing in the photograph that confirms exactly what is in the envelope. It could be a birthday card. And if Frank comes back with some sort of proof that he was conducting an undercover operation...well, it's a tricky, thin line."

Reece released her from his embrace and dialed the number. Joe answered on the first ring. "I wasn't sure this number would work. I guess this number doesn't belong to the cell phone you left in my car."

"And speaking of my cell phone, what did you do with it?"

"I removed the GPS chip and smashed it. Everything else is in the glove compartment of my car. Just because I didn't want you tracking me doesn't mean I was willing to let someone else get hold of your phone and its memory."

"I appreciate that consideration. So, what can I do for you at this late hour? Surely you aren't wanting to set up a midnight meeting somewhere, are you? I do happen to know the location of a twenty-four-hour grocery store."

A knowing chuckle escaped Reece's throat. "So do I." His manner quickly turned to business. "Did you come up with anything on the ballistics check?"

"I sure did. Two unsolved murders, both matching the markings on the spent cartridge you gave me."

"Who, when and where?"

"Coincidentally, both occurred in Rocky Shores but were about six months apart without any direct connection between the two victims other than the murder weapon. Both incidents were written up as probable gang activity, a straightforward robbery gone bad."

"Do you think you could tie the victims together through association with some of Mitch Mantee's dealings?"

"I have some people working on that angle right now." Joe sucked in an audible breath, then expelled it. "I think we've come to the end of this little game of yours, Reece. You've now been apprised that the weapon in your possession was involved in two murders. If I don't know everything you know by the end of this conversation, we're talking an arrest warrant for withholding information."

"But two local murders wouldn't be federal jurisdiction."

"It would be if we tie the victims to Mitch Mantee. I don't know what kind of a mess you're in or who this friend of yours is, although I suspect your friend is currently using the alias of Trixie. But I do know that if you've stumbled on some kind of a connection between Frank James and Mitch Mantee, then you're in way over your head. You need my help and I need to know what you know. This might have started out for you as helping a friend with a stalking situation, but you and I both know that it's escalated way beyond that and beyond your ability to handle it alone."

There was a long pause while Reece gathered his thoughts. He knew Joe was serious in his threat to get an arrest warrant. He also knew that everything Joe said was true.

"You're right. This has grown much bigger and more complex than either my friend or I ever thought it could. We never suspected that her being stalked was only the tip of the iceberg and would lead to Frank James and ultimately to Mitch Mantee."

"Ah, so you admit that your friend is a *her* rather than a him. Then I was right in my assumption about Trixie? And what would Trixie's real name be?"

"Well...it's Brandi—"

"Knock it off, Reece." Joe snapped out an irritated answer. "I want some real answers, not more games."

"Oddly enough, that's the truth."

"Brandi what?"

Reece paused for a moment, then continued cautiously. "I don't like talking about this on a cell phone that's not equipped with security features. Anything that travels the airwaves rather than phone lines can be easily intercepted. Anyone can come across the right frequency by accident and be able to listen in on our conversation."

"Okay. Where and when do you want to meet?"

"Tomorrow morning...seven o'clock in Seattle at the Pergola in Pioneer Square. Brandi will not be there, and if I don't return to her location by a designated time, she'll know what to do."

Joe disconnected the call and returned his attention to his computer. He glanced at his colleague. "We've got to find a location on Reece Covington immediately. I want everyone and everything connected to his past run through the computer. Somehow we've missed something. Keep in mind that he was the best private investigator around and did a lot of work for various high-dollar defense attorneys and also for various local law enforcement agencies. Prosecutors were willing to work with him because he never provided his services to anyone defending known organized crime figures or even local big-name criminals. His defense attorney work was usually in civil cases rather than criminal ones. One of the services he provided was hiding the occasional surprise witness until the trial. There has to be someplace where he could take them without creating any suspicion or being concerned about someone leaking the information. We've got to find that place."

"We've checked utilities, property tax, credit cards, banks...there's nothing on him since his release from prison. It's like he ceased to exist. If it weren't for his phone calls, I'd say he had become a nonperson. I'm not finding anything on property ownership since he sold his house on Mercer Island. It's almost like he's living in a cave or a tree house—something without an address or utilities. Maybe he's literally living out of his car, moving from one place to another each night."

"You are running those car tags, aren't you? I'm sure anything of his that is as visible as a vehicle will be hidden behind all manner of diversions. He might be living someplace that's in someone else's name. Dig back through his family. Go clear back to the day he was born if that's what you need to do, but do it quickly."

Joe glanced at his watch. Less than twelve hours to solve the complex riddle of Reece Covington and some woman named Brandi. "What about that other matter?"

"We have twenty-four-hour surveillance and have the court-ordered phone taps."

Joe clenched his jaw in determination. Frank James worked for the Rocky Shores police. Reece used to have an office in Rocky Shores. Somehow some woman named Brandi had gotten on Frank's bad side. And somehow this woman and Reece had a connection. Could the town of Rocky Shores be the common denominator between Frank, Reece and Brandi?

Joe started a computer search of utilities for someone with a first name of Brandi living in Rocky Shores. If she worked in Rocky Shores but lived elsewhere, he would be back at square one again. Hopefully he would get lucky. If he came up with a name, then he could run it through the driver's license pictures and see if he could find a match for the woman who was with Reece. He was due for a little good luck for a change.

And he was running out of time.

REECE LAY IN BED WITH BRANDI wrapped in his arms. They enjoyed the peaceful moments of blissful contentment following lovemaking, an oasis of calm in the midst of chaos.

She continued to draw from his strength. There was no doubt in her mind that she had fallen in love with him. One week ago she hadn't even known he existed, and now he was the most important person in her life. But how real was it? Had she mistaken her gratitude to him for love? And how did he feel about her? He had risked his life to protect her, but that didn't mean it was love. It could have been nothing more than his desire to redeem his own past.

His voice interrupted her thoughts. "I've gone through all our options, and I see only one viable choice. So, unless Joe says or does something tomorrow morning that changes my mind, I'm going to fill him in on everything we know and see what Joe can do about getting you some protection."

He placed a loving kiss on her lips. "This has escalated to the point where I can't guarantee your safety. My ownership of this cabin is well hidden, but the longer someone keeps at it the more likely they are to find it, even if only by accident."

He drew in a steadying breath as he sat up in bed with his back against the headboard. "Take a look around. It's like I've created our own little prison here—thermal imaging surveillance cameras for perimeter monitoring, checking my car for tracking devices, clandestine meetings, secrecy. It's like we're involved in some kind of a standoff that started out as us and them, with the *them* being Frank James. Then I involved the FBI by contacting a friend of mine, which seemed like a good idea at the time. But now that has become a second *them.* Then the original *them* became a whole lot larger and much more dangerous when we discovered a major organized crime figure was involved."

He pulled her into his arms and held her tightly. "When I was released from prison, all I wanted to do was hide away. But I've realized over the past few days that I don't want that type of isolation. I want to put the past behind me and get on with my life. I don't see any way that we can put an end to this predicament by ourselves, and continuing like this is certainly not fair to you. So, unless you have some valid objection, that's what I think would be best. Are you going to be okay with that?"

"I'm not sure what to think. When you say federal protection, are you talking about the witness protection thing where they give me a new identity and I disappear from everything I've ever known?" Would it be a situation where she would never be allowed to see Reece again? She didn't like that idea at all.

"There wouldn't be any reason for me to be in protective custody. The only thing I know is what's in those two photographs—and you've seen them, too. And so has my agent. And your P.I. friend has copies of them, although you didn't tell him what was in them. All the

FBI would need from me is a deposition saying that I took the photographs, where and when. Once they have that, there's nothing else I can say or do that would be of any danger to anyone. I couldn't even testify to what the people in the picture were doing beyond what it looked like. I have no firsthand knowledge. I didn't even see them arrive at or depart from the location, and I don't know how long they were there. Once the information has been passed on, I'm not a threat to anyone."

"That doesn't mean they won't be out for revenge." Reece had purposely stayed away from crystallizing his feelings about Brandi. He didn't want the emotion to interfere with what needed to be done. But the possibility of never seeing her again...well, he may not have wanted to admit it to himself, but he knew it would break his heart. He would have to be content with knowing that she was safe. If anything happened to her because of his selfishness in wanting to bring down Frank James, he knew he wouldn't be able to live with it.

"I'll agree to you telling Joe everything if you think that's best, but I won't live my life cut off from everything and everyone I've ever known while stuck away in some safe little corner with a new name and identity."

"When I mentioned Joe providing protection for you, I was only thinking about an interim period until they had everything under control." He heard the sob she tried to suppress and saw the anguish that covered her like a blanket. It touched his heart as nothing else ever had.

"Oh, Brandi...hopefully I'm making this seem more

dire than it really is rather than the other way around. I don't want you to disappear from my—"

The sound of the alarm cut through the air. Brandi's body stiffened to full alert. Her eyes went wide as she looked to Reece.

A hard jolt of adrenaline pumped through his veins. He jumped into immediate action, giving orders as he pulled on a pair of sweatpants and grabbed his pistol.

"Get some clothes on, then stay hidden between the bed and the wall. I'll be right back."

She responded immediately, doing as she had been instructed. Her pulse raced and her mouth went dry. Her heart pounded loudly enough that she thought she could hear it. Had all their fears and concerns finally caught up with them? Had Frank James located them? Was a professional hit man just outside the cabin?

And then the most abstract thought of all—she had never had the opportunity to tell Reece that she loved him. She watched as he jammed his feet into his boots while checking the monitors on the table. He seemed to be staring at something, but she couldn't tell what it was.

Reece tried to decipher the exact meaning of the images showing up on the monitor. There was a vehicle parked on the fire road and two people standing about ten feet off the road toward the cabin. The two people weren't going anywhere. From the stance of the images, it appeared that they were talking and occasionally pointing at something. He heard the rain as it started to hit against the roof, which coincided with the two images returning to the vehicle and slowly driving away.

It was at that moment that he realized he had been

holding his breath. A professional hit man would not be deterred by rain. He would use it to his advantage to mask his trail and cover any sounds that would alert the occupants of the cabin to his presence.

Reece relaxed a little. Perhaps it was nothing more than coincidence. Maybe someone who was lost and trying to get his bearings. Possibly even someone in need of relieving himself who stopped by the edge of the road since there weren't any public bathroom facilities in the area. Whoever had been there was gone.

At least for the time being.

Chapter Eleven

Reece huddled against the rain as he waited in the doorway of the closed shop across the street from the Pioneer Square Pergola. He checked his watch. Five minutes until seven—four minutes and fifty-nine seconds before Joe Hodges would miraculously appear from wherever he had stationed himself. He scanned the surrounding area. He could almost feel Joe's eyes on him. The FBI agent had probably picked a spot in the parking garage down the block, binoculars in hand.

Reece normally wouldn't have allowed himself to be so exposed, but he had told Joe that he had a backup plan in place if he was taken into custody. He stifled a yawn. He had gotten up at four-thirty that morning in order to be able to meet Joe at seven o'clock. The sounding of the alarm on the monitoring system had set the tone for the rest of the night. Even though nothing of consequence had happened, he had not gotten very much sleep. It seemed as if he had been awake most of the night, only occasionally dozing off until the clock had turned to four-thirty.

And now it had come down to his third face-to-face

meeting with Joe Hodges in less than a week—and most likely the last one, at least under these conditions of secrecy.

"Right on time, I see." Joe's voice broke into his thoughts. He had been so absorbed that he hadn't been aware of Joe approaching him. It was a bad sign, one that told him he had lost his edge and perspective on what was going on. Definitely time to share the secrets with someone else. Hopefully he was placing his trust in the right person.

Hopefully Joe was that right person.

Reece acknowledged Joe's presence with a nod. "We should have met someplace not quite so wet."

"This location was your choice. How about the coffee shop down the street? We can get some breakfast, some hot coffee and try to dry out."

Reece shot Joe a questioning look. "Someplace you've already staked out and covered?"

"Then pick a place more to your liking. I was only thinking of what would be close."

Reece took a steadying breath in an attempt to settle his nerves and calm his uncertainties. He didn't like the sensation of not having control, and there was no doubt in his mind that the situation had been spiraling out of control faster than he could keep up with it.

"The coffee shop is fine. It doesn't matter whether or not you have it covered."

"Well, that's quite a change in attitude. You've decided to throw caution to the wind?"

"Not at all. What I have done is make the decision to fill you in on exactly what's going on."

Joe flashed a teasing grin. "That's a pleasant surprise."

The two men walked the half block to the coffee shop and sat in a back booth. Reece insisted on facing the door so he could see who was coming and going. They ordered breakfast and engaged in casual conversation about the weather and sports until the waitress brought them their food. As soon as she was out of earshot, Joe wasted no time in getting down to the business at hand.

"Where did you get that Beretta pistol, and where is it now? As I told you, I've tied it to a couple of murders so far."

"As to where it is…I have it hidden in a secure location along with some other pertinent evidence. It's safe and I can testify that its chain of custody is unbroken and uncompromised from the person who had it to where it is now."

"You know you'll have to turn it over to me. The ballistics sample you gave me allowed me to make a match, but without the actual weapon is doesn't carry much weight. What is the other evidence you mentioned? And how does Miss Doyle fit into this?"

The shock hit Reece quicker than he was able to cover his surprise. "How did you know—"

"You've been leading me on a merry chase. It's been a long time since someone tested my ability to think outside the box. It was a good refresher course."

Reece immediately latched on to the way Joe was avoiding any additional mention of Brandi. Joe had dropped the bomb in letting him know that he had discovered her identity, then abandoned that topic of conversation. He recognized the tactic and grudgingly admired the irony. It was the exact same thing he had done to Joe when he threw in Mitch Mantee's name just before terminating their phone conversation.

He decided to play it Joe's way for the moment. "That tracking bug you slipped inside my car in addition to your cell phone was a clever maneuver."

"I thought so, too. But you found it much quicker than I assumed you would. And planting it on a delivery truck rather than destroying it was definitely a stroke of brilliance. Just for future reference, what made you look for something else that soon?"

"You did. We were supposed to meet inside the grocery store, yet when I pulled up alongside you and told you to get in, you didn't offer even one word of objection, a moment's hesitation or even suggest a compromise."

"Let's have the rest of it, Reece. You've already been told that you're withholding information in a crime by continuing to hold on to the Beretta and not divulging any information about who it belongs to and how it came to be in your possession, yet you're still playing cat and mouse with me. What is so important that you're willing to risk a return trip to prison?"

Reece clenched his jaw in determination, but couldn't stop the frown that wrinkled across his forehead. "What do you know about Brandi, other than having tracked down her identity?"

"There isn't anything much to know. Professional photographer of weddings and portraits, pays her bills on time, no unusual indebtedness, no apparent bad habits, no known unsavory associates, absolutely nothing on her in any law enforcement database—not even a traffic ticket. All in all, the type of person who leads a quiet law-abiding life. Other than the fact that she lives and works in Rocky Shores, I can't find any connection between her and Frank James. So, what does she have to do with a murder weapon, and why would Frank James be stalking her? I don't see the connection."

Reece stared at his coffee cup as he raced through his options. He leveled a steady look at Joe, making and holding eye contact. "All right. Here it is."

Joe leaned back in his seat as he expelled a sigh of relief. "Finally. I was afraid you were going to make me wrestle you to the ground in order to force the information out of you. Let's start with you telling me where Miss Doyle is."

"No, let's *don't* start there. I'll tell you what's going on, but I'm not going to compromise her location without some guarantees from you regarding her safety, and, of course, she has to agree to accept your offer."

"Okay, start talking."

"As you noted, Brandi is a professional photographer. But what you don't know is that in addition to weddings and portraits, she's spent the past several months doing location photography for a coffee-table-type book of scenic pictures showing the beauty of the state of Washington. It's two of those pictures that's the cause of all her trouble, starting with Frank James stalking her."

Joe jerked upright, his attention riveted on what

Reece was saying. "Photographs…she took a picture of something she wasn't supposed to? Was she trying to blackmail someone?"

"Slow down, Joe. You're jumping to a very wrong conclusion. She didn't have any idea what she had done, what she had accidentally captured on film. She didn't know why someone would be stalking her. She didn't even know the identity of her stalker until after I became involved."

Reece unfolded the entire story, giving Joe all the details except the information about his cabin and the name and location of his friend who had the backup evidence. "So, that's what is going on. A photograph of Frank James in an isolated setting being handed an envelope by Mitch Mantee in what appears to be a payoff. Cindy Thatcher is present in one of the photos, and there's another man in the other photograph with his back to the camera. I'm assuming he's one of Mitch's bodyguards."

"And the Beretta came directly from Frank's hand?"

"Yep, fingerprints still intact on the pistol and most likely on the cartridges in the magazine. It holds eight shots. One of them went off when we struggled for the pistol, and it caught a piece of Frank. I have his blood on my jacket, and I'm sure there's some blow-back on the barrel of the pistol. I test-fired two more shots, one for you to check out and the other sent out of state to be held as backup security. There are still five cartridges remaining in the magazine."

"I want the pistol and the photographs. Where are they? How and when do I get them?"

"First, I want some guarantees for Brandi's safety. She's being stalked by a rogue cop who went so far as to abduct her. That's pretty heavy duty, especially since she can identify him. But it's also only her word against his. And now Mitch Mantee is involved. With that, we're talking the possibility of a professional hit man… *if* Mitch is aware of what has happened. I question how much of this Frank has actually conveyed to Mitch. For his own safety, he might be trying to contain it and handle it himself, which would explain the stalking and finally the abduction."

"A valid point."

"As far as court is concerned, the only thing she can testify to that involves Mitch is that she took the photographs in question but had no knowledge of the significance of what she accidentally caught in the background and did not know the identity of any of the people at the time she took the picture. But Frank abducting her is another matter."

Joe nodded his head in agreement. "Yes, that's a different legal problem."

"Don't bother to tell me all the *problems.* I already know them and so does Brandi. When she tried to report the stalking, the Rocky Shores police dismissed her story and did not make a report. She never had an opportunity to report the abduction, which means there's no police report on that, either. She wasn't taken across a state line so there's nothing federal there. So, it all comes down to what guarantees you can give for her safety."

"At this moment, until I check with the Bureau, the

only thing I can give you is my personal guarantee that I will do everything I can to keep her safe."

The moment of truth had arrived. Everything came down to whether Reece was willing to put his trust in Joe Hodges. He leveled a steady gaze at Joe, then finally reached his hand across the table. His tone of voice left no confusion about his meaning. "Brandi is very important to me. I'm holding you to that promise."

Joe accepted his handshake. "You have my word."

Reece picked up the bill for their breakfast and handed it to Joe while flashing a teasing grin. "I haven't found a job yet, so I guess we're still on your expense account."

"If the cost of breakfast gets me a piece of Mitch Mantee, then it's well worth it."

Reece started to stand up, but Joe stopped him. "Hold on. We're not finished. Where and when do I get the Beretta, the pictures and a formal introduction to Miss Doyle so that she and I can have a for-the-record conversation?"

"You haven't told me how you intend to protect Brandi. None of this goes down unless she agrees to trust your word."

"As far as the federal case against Mitch Mantee, we'll take her deposition about the photographs. That should be enough so that she won't be required to testify in court. The other situation with Frank James is a local matter. However, by being able to tie Frank to Mitch Mantee, we can extend protection to her. I can put her in a safe house until Frank's trial."

Joe stared at Reece, obviously sorting something

through his mind. "You said you struggled with Frank and he caught a piece of a bullet before you took the pistol away from him, that you have his blood on your jacket."

"Yes, that's what happened."

"*Where* did it happen?"

"Inside Brandi's house. We had gone there to search through her files to determine what else was missing other than the negatives and prints originally stolen from her files. Frank must have been watching her house in case we returned to complete what we had started the previous night, when he had almost caught us. He entered the house as we were preparing to leave. I struggled with him in her living room. If the wound was a through-and-through, the slug is still somewhere in her house along with his blood."

"That ties it all together very neatly...photograph of Frank with Mitch, Brandi's claim of stalking and abduction by Frank verified by his blood inside her house, the Beretta tied to Frank by more than just your testimony and his fingerprints on the weapon. The recovery of the bullet from her house will verify that. Lots of forensic evidence."

"I'll give you a call after I've had an opportunity to discuss all of this with Brandi. I'll let you know if she agrees to your offer of a safe house and making herself available to you. Either way, I'll deliver the photographs and the Beretta to you later today."

"Agreed."

Reece stood up, then paused before leaving. "It really doesn't seem fair, does it?"

"What?"

"Brandi is the innocent bystander who, through no fault of her own, became embroiled in the middle of a nightmare involving a dirty cop and a crime boss, yet she's the one who will be confined while the bad guys are walking around free. You know something? I'm not so sure she'll go for that, and speaking for myself, I couldn't blame her."

"You're right. It's not fair. I see a lot of things that are not fair in my daily routine."

"Don't worry…you'll get your evidence. I'll turn over the Beretta and the pictures either way, but I can't speak for Brandi."

Reece left the coffee shop. Even though he and Joe had come to an agreement, he still didn't want to be tracked to his cabin. He wanted the location to remain hidden. He pulled the meter from his pocket and checked his vehicle for any tracking devices. When he was satisfied that it was clean, he headed back to his cabin. He kept a watchful eye on his rearview mirror, just in case.

As soon as he arrived, he sat down with Brandi and related the details of his meeting with Joe. "That's the deal. Until Joe checks with the Bureau he can't offer you anything official, but he has given his personal word to see that you're protected until Frank's trial. Joe didn't specifically say so, but I got the impression from him that your involvement in anything having to do directly with Mitch Mantee would be minimal. He indicated that he didn't believe you would be in any danger from mob reprisal after the fact and that protection before the trial would be a formality rather than a necessity."

He brushed a tender kiss across her lips. "What do you think? I told Joe I'd call him this afternoon and let him know what you want to do about a safe house."

"The only thing that's really up in the air is whether I present myself, give them a deposition about the photographs and agree to testify if they need me to?"

"Yes, as far as Mitch Mantee is concerned. Turning over the photographs and the pistol are no longer in question. That has to be done and I agreed to it." He pulled her into his embrace. "But Frank James is a different matter. The abduction charges, if the prosecution chooses to go ahead with that part of the case, would rely solely on your testimony."

She searched his face, finally settling on his eyes. "Do you trust Joe's word? He did manage to identify me very quickly from nothing more than my first name and having seen me once. Do you think he already knows where this cabin is?"

"It's possible...anything is possible. It's also possible that Frank James has managed to stumble across this, too. As far as trusting Joe, I've never known him to go back on his word when it's been accompanied by his handshake."

She took in a deep breath, held it for several seconds, then slowly exhaled. "Apparently our little adventure has come to its conclusion. Call Joe and tell him we'll both be there. However—" she sucked in a deep breath to settle her rattled nerves "—I won't be locked away in some safe house where I'll feel like I'm the one in prison. I can't live my life that way."

"Are you sure? This has to be your decision. I'm willing to testify to my involvement and what I discovered, but this is too critical for me to make the decision for you."

She extended a confident smile. "I'm sure. Call Joe."

"You won't be alone. I'll be with you every step of the way."

His reassuring words about being with her sent a warm sensation washing through her body. The end was in sight, a positive conclusion to a nightmare that was unlike anything she had ever imagined being involved in.

And the beginning of a new life that included Reece Covington? That was something still to be determined, a subject that she knew she couldn't broach until everything else was resolved. She watched as he dialed Joe's number.

"Joe...Brandi has agreed to do whatever needs to be done, but refused to be shut away in some safe house. We'll meet you..." He glanced at his watch. It was only eleven o'clock, not even noon yet. He didn't want to meet with Joe until close to dinner time. "At five o'clock at the same grocery store in Bellevue. I'll have the pistol and photographs with me." By waiting until a time when people were going home from work, stopping at the store, the activity level would be higher than mid-afternoon. Should anything go wrong, they would have a better chance of disappearing in a crowd.

FRANK JAMES PUNCHED THE speed dial button on his phone. The excitement surged through his veins. His words came out machine-gun fast. "I've found it. There's a cabin in the Cascade Mountains, an hour or two from here. The title shows Reece's mother's maiden name. Same with the utilities. The only problem with that is that his mother died ten years ago. That has to be where he's hiding and where he has the Doyle woman. In fact, that's probably the connection between them. The cabin is very close to where she escaped from my car."

"Whoa...slow down, Frank. You're talking faster than I can keep up with it. You've located a cabin a couple of hours from here that appears to actually be owned by Reece regardless of the name on the title and the deed?"

"Right. That's got to be where he's been hiding and where he's got the Doyle woman stashed. Let's go get her."

"Calm down, Frank. We're not going to storm the cabin without doing a little reconnaissance first. We have to verify that he's there. Requisition a police helicopter. Use the excuse that you're checking a tip from an informant about a drug deal. I'll meet you at the hangar in an hour. We'll do a flyover of the area and see if we can spot his vehicle and determine if the cabin is occupied."

"I have a map of the area. There's a fire road directly behind the cabin with easy access to the paved road through that section."

"Good. That will give us a place to set down if it

comes to that. My preference is to take a couple of your men and quietly sneak in by car rather than the noise of a copter."

"I'll see you in an hour." Frank disconnected the call, then made arrangements for the helicopter. As soon as everything was arranged, he forced his attention to the report he had been working on. He needed to finish it up before going to the hangar. He worked for a few minutes, but it was no good. He couldn't focus his attention anywhere other than the possibility of being able to handle Reece Covington again. Resolving his problem with Brandi and her photographs was almost incidental at the moment. The nervous energy took its toll on his composure.

He had been working almost nonstop on the problem of locating Reece. One way or the other, his nemesis was not going to come out of this alive. Without Reece, the question of his confiscated Beretta wouldn't come to light. And the last thing he needed was for anyone to know about that little fiasco.

Especially Mitch Mantee.

Frank left the police station and drove to the hangar. He checked with the pilot and indicated on the map where the area was that they wanted to check. Then he nervously paced up and down as he waited.

He looked up to see the man walking through the door. "It's about time. Let's go."

The two men climbed into the helicopter along with the pilot. A minute later they were in the air and headed toward the mountains. They followed the fire road in from the paved road until Frank pointed toward the ground. "There...that has to be it."

He turned toward the pilot. "Can you get around to a place where we can see inside that carport to check it for a vehicle?"

"I think so, Lieutenant." He maneuvered to the other side of the cabin, being ever mindful of the tall trees as he descended to a level where the inside of the carport was visible.

A surge of excitement grabbed Frank James. There it was, the SUV he had finally been able to trace to Reece Covington. "Look...his vehicle in the carport and smoke coming from the chimney." Mindful of the pilot's presence, he was careful with his words. "This confirms our tip. Let's head back."

After they landed, the pilot went to the hangar office to fill in his log book. Frank and his most important colleague went to the parking lot, where they could talk in private.

"Nice job, Frank. Get two of your most trusted men and meet me—" he pointed to a specific coordinate on the map close to Reece's cabin "—right here at two-thirty. You'll need to hurry. It's almost noon now. That doesn't give you much time."

Frank furrowed his brow in a moment's confusion. "Do you think it's wise for you to be there?"

He leveled a stern warning at Frank. "You've bungled this little problem twice. I'm not leaving it in your hands for a third attempt."

Frank watched as the figure disappeared around the corner of the hangar. A moment later he saw the car pull out of the parking lot. That cinched it. He had to make sure that Reece Covington would not have an opportunity to say anything that could cause him any repercussions. It was down to the wire. First and foremost, he had to look out for his own safety and well being.

Brandi Doyle was an inconvenience. But Reece Covington was a serious threat to his existence and had to be dealt with.

Permanently.

Chapter Twelve

Joe Hodges swiveled around in his chair until he faced one of his men. The large office looked more like a command center than anything else. "What's happening with that surveillance?"

"It's in place and working. Here's a report of what's been happening so far." The agent handed Joe a computer printout.

Joe took the report and glanced through it, paying closer attention to the pertinent details that caught his attention. He poured himself another cup of coffee, took a sip and set the mug on his desk. The nervous energy continued to shove at him, fueled by the excessive amounts of caffeine he had consumed since early that morning. "I don't like it. We still don't have the complete picture. This should be straightforward, especially now that I know what it is that Reece has and the woman's connection to it. In fact, if the Doyle woman had come to us originally—"

"From what you've said of your last meeting with Covington, it doesn't sound like she had an opportunity to contact us. And at the time, all she could do was say she had been abducted. She apparently didn't have any knowledge of the implications of the people in the background of her photographs."

Joe took another swallow from his coffee mug. "Yes...I suppose that's right. But for some reason Reece is still playing it very cagey. There's something we don't know, something he's holding back from me. He still seems to be very concerned about her safety. I even went out on a limb and guaranteed her protection until the trial, although I don't see any need for her personal testimony against Mitch Mantee. Her deposition saying she took the photographs in question and the reason she took them, which had no connection to the identity of the people caught in the background, is really her only involvement with that."

"But if Frank James is the one who abducted her, she is the one and only eyewitness as well as being the victim. That should be an area of concern for her."

"Yes, and there's the added fact that Reece certainly has a history with Frank James. It was the lieutenant's direct testimony that put Reece in prison, testimony Reece claims was perjury."

"Do you think he was really railroaded?"

Joe furrowed his brow in a moment of concentration. "I think there's a good chance that it went down the way Reece says it did. But that's not within our jurisdiction." His concentration turned to a scowl. "There's something else going on here. We don't have the complete picture. And knowing Reece, whatever it is that we're missing is somehow pertinent to the overall picture. The primary question is whether Reece is holding back information for personal reasons based on his past relationship with Frank or if it's something new and relevant to the current situation."

He picked up a piece of paper from his desk. "This list of the items Reece purchased at the electronic supply store tells us he's expecting trouble, but exactly what and from whom? Is it just extra precautions he's taking against Frank James or is there more? As long as I've known Reece, I've never been able to really read him. He always gives the impression that there's so much more going on inside him than he lets anyone see. It's very difficult to second-guess a person like that. You always feel like you're playing catch-up rather than ever being ahead of him."

"Why don't we just pick him up?"

"He's already agreed to present himself to us later today so he can turn over the pistol and the photographs. Logistically we can't really pick him up any sooner than the time we're supposed to meet. Besides, we have no reason to pick him up. He hasn't violated any federal laws."

Joe grabbed his coffee mug and took another swallow. He shook his head in resignation as he mumbled more to himself than to anyone else in the room. "He would have made a terrific FBI agent—good instincts and very resourceful." Then he clenched his jaw. "Actually, he wouldn't. He's not a team player. He would never follow the rules."

He glanced out the window. "Damn...looks like it's about to rain again. We sure don't need that."

REECE CHECKED THE TIME. "We'd better get ready." He turned toward Brandi, noting the hint of anxiety that flashed across her face. "Are you sure you want to go with me—to expose yourself to FBI questioning?"

"Yes. Even though I don't want Joe to hide me away somewhere, that doesn't mean that I'm not willing to answer whatever questions he might have or cooperate in any way I can with his investigation. Besides, if we are accompanied by FBI agents, then there won't be any danger in going to my house to search for the bullet that wounded Frank and taking samples of any blood we might find. That way the FBI can claim undisturbed custody of that evidence, and we can prove that Frank was inside my house without my permission or a warrant."

"I didn't mention anything to Joe about going to your house."

A hint of a smile tugged at the corners of her mouth. "I'll bet if you offer him that opportunity and tell him why, he won't have any objections to taking the time."

He pulled her into his embrace, gazed lovingly into her eyes, then placed a tender kiss on her lips. He closed his eyes as he cradled her head against his shoulder and drew in a steadying breath. "When this is over I want to sit down with you and have a serious talk about the future."

A nervous energy jittered inside her. "I look forward to it." But did he want to talk about the same thing that she wanted to hear? About a future they could share? Or did he intend to gracefully let her down and explain why it would never work? That it had been an exciting adventure, but not something that could be the basis for a lifetime? She loved him. That was an absolute fact. But the future left her uncertain and anxiety-ridden. He held her a moment longer, the warmth of his arms once again filling her with a sense that everything would be all right.

He finally let go of her. "We need to get ready for our meeting with Joe." He did a quick glance at the security monitors, as he had done every few minutes. Then he turned his attention toward the items he had spread out on the sofa. Prints of the photographs—both the original pictures where the people in the background were discernable but not recognizable, then the blowups of the section with the people in the background so that their faces were clearly shown. A sealed plastic bag containing the .25-caliber Beretta Bobcat pistol and a detailed description of how he came to be in possession of the pistol and who it belonged to.

And last, but not least, he checked the magazine of his own 9 mm pistol, reinserted it into the handle, loaded a cartridge into the chamber, then placed the pistol in the holster.

She looked at him curiously, her concern obvious in her tone of voice. "Are you going to take that with you to meet an FBI agent? Won't that be risky if something happens and he decides to search you?"

"I'm not feeling very confident about any of this. Something—call it instinct if you want—is nagging at me. We're missing something, but I don't know what it is. I don't want to be caught unprepared."

He placed his laptop computer into its carrying case,

then stuck the flash drive into an outside pocket of the case. "And to that end I want to copy the files and e-mails sent to me by your agent, both the original scanning of all twelve photographs and the rescanning of the two pertinent ones. That will also show the nature of the photographs you had been taking and how the two in question fit into that series and that what you had captured was obviously accidental, making you an innocent bystander. I'll transfer the material to the flash drive with Joe as a witness, then turn the flash drive over to him."

"That should take care of everything."

He heard her words, but the apprehension in the depths of her eyes told him something else. Over the past few days his priorities had changed dramatically. Helping Brandi as a means of settling an old score with Frank James was no longer the primary focus of his efforts. She was now his main concern. It had all happened so quickly, but he knew that she meant more to him than any other person he had ever known. He would do everything in his power to keep her safe, and if that meant another physical confrontation with Frank James, then that's what would happen.

He loved her. There was no other way to say it, no other way to think about it. Straightforward and simple—he loved Brandi Doyle. And when their nightmare was finally over… The thought trailed off. Unless he was able to clear his record he had nothing to offer her. True, he had a lot of money stashed away from the sale of his Mercer Island house, but he no longer had a career or any positive direction for the future. He couldn't expect her to make a commitment to a man who had nothing to offer and didn't even know what path his future would take.

Nothing to offer other than his love.

He shook the thoughts from his head. This wasn't the time or the place. They had a meeting and needed to be on the road. It had started raining again. He wanted to allow some extra travel time.

The sound of the monitor alarm grabbed his attention. A quick jolt of trepidation raced through his body. He shot a quick glance at Brandi, then checked the monitor. A car had stopped on the fire road, and three people emerged from the vehicle. He switched the monitor from the thermal imaging camera to a regular camera. An image of Frank James popped onto the screen.

"We've got to get the hell out of here now!"

Reece's tone of voice and clipped words told Brandi everything she needed to know. They were in trouble. She grabbed her purse and tucked the envelope containing the photographs inside her jacket to protect them from the rain. Reece slung the strap of his computer case over his head and across his chest. He shoved the plastic bag containing the Beretta into an inside jacket pocket. Then he grabbed his holstered 9 mm pistol and clipped it to the waistband of his jeans at the small of his back and covered it with his sweatshirt.

"Stay with me. We're going to head into the woods, then circle back to the car while they're running around looking for us."

They charged out to the front porch. He paused just

long enough to pull the door shut. He heard the lock click. "If they want inside my cabin, they're going to have to take the time to break in." They bolted down the front steps and headed toward the cover of the forest with its trees and underbrush.

The voice came toward them from the direction of the fire road. "There they go. Don't let them get away!"

Brandi's heart lodged in her throat. A shot rang out. Her heart pounded wildly. She heard the bullet hit a tree not more than five feet from her. It took all her willpower to keep her panic shoved aside. It was as if she had been transported back in time by six days. There she was, running through the woods in the rain. Running for her life again. Her shoes digging into the mud as she raced forward trying to escape her pursuer. Only this time the pursuer was truly on her heels, and he was shooting at her.

Reece had a firm grasp on her hand as he led the way. The rain increased to a drenching downpour. The pelting raindrops stung her face and obscured her vision as they ran into her eyes. She gasped for air, wondering if each lung full would be her last.

She lost her traction and fought to maintain her balance, but to no avail. A moment later she landed on her rear end in the mud, jerking Reece to an abrupt halt. He quickly scanned the woods, seeking any hint of where their pursuers were. He caught a quick glimpse of two men who seemed a little uncertain about which direction to go in.

He pulled Brandi to her feet. "Are you okay?"

"Yes. Let's go."

They took off running again. Another two hundred yards and Reece pulled her down between some large rocks and thick brush so that they were concealed from all sides. He sucked in several deep breaths in an effort to force some calm to his breathing. Brandi did the same.

They continued to watch from their hiding place, straining to see any little movement among the trees or catch a glimpse of the color of clothing. His words were a raspy whisper in her ear. "We'll stay here for a little bit until we know that whoever is out there has continued on so that we're behind them rather than in front. Then we can circle back to the cabin and get the car. Once we're on the road I'll be able to lose whoever is foolish enough to try and follow us."

Reece felt Brandi's muscles tense as the two men came into view. He immediately recognized one of them as Frank James. Neither he nor Brandi moved or spoke as the two men made their way through the underbrush. A flicker of satisfaction ignited inside Reece. It was obvious that their pursuers didn't know much about mountains and forests or about how to track someone while being inconspicuous. One of them was even wearing a bright red jacket—fine if he was a hunter and wanted to be seen by other hunters for his own protection, but stupid if he was trying to trail someone through the woods.

He watched as the two men conferred, then split up and went in different directions. They continued to move away from the cabin and farther into the woods.

He kept his eye on them until they had disappeared from sight.

He tugged on her hand. "Come on. Let's go. Stay down as low as you can and keep your eyes open. We only saw Frank and one other man. The third one may be out here, too, or he may have stayed behind in case we doubled back. We need to be on the lookout for him."

Brandi sucked in a steadying breath in an attempt to still her tattered nerves. They started back toward the cabin. He continued to keep her hand firmly clasped in his, providing her with the confidence that told her everything would work out. She had faith in him. She trusted him implicitly.

They ran as fast as the muddy ground allowed. He slowed the pace as they neared the cabin, then stopped when they were within fifty feet of the carport. They hid from sight of anyone around the cabin or his vehicle. The front door of the cabin was still closed and appeared to be intact rather than looking as if anyone had kicked it in. He carefully scrutinized the area, ever mindful of the third person who had arrived in the vehicle on the fire road—a third person whose location was unknown.

He tugged on her hand, pulling her close so that she could hear his whispered words. "We can't wait any longer. If we stay here trying to spot the third person, it will give the other two enough time to realize we doubled back. We need to make a break for the carport." He squeezed her hand. "Are you ready?"

She returned the squeeze. "Let's go."

The tension knotted in his stomach. Everything was

on the line. Once they were in the car and out on the fire road, the immediate danger would be behind them. Once they were on the road he would be able to lose whoever was following them. He corrected the thought. Once they were on the road he would be able to lose Frank James. Then as soon as they turned their evidence over to Joe Hodges, the FBI would take Frank into custody. The nightmare would be over.

He sucked in a calming breath, then they left the safety of underbrush concealing them. They made a dash across the clearing toward his SUV. He continually scanned the area, searching for any sign of the third man. As soon as they reached the carport, he pulled his keys from his pocket and clicked the door unlock button. Safety was only a moment away.

"Hold it right there, Covington."

The words sent a deathly chill slicing through Brandi's body. She whirled around and saw the man step from behind the corner of the carport…holding a shotgun. She didn't know who he was, but one glance at Reece told her he recognized the man.

Reece's voice held an eerie calm, belying the tension she felt coursing through her body. Every muscle seemed to be drawn into taut, hard lines. "Lyle Hanover. This certainly explains a lot. Now all the pieces are in place. Frank James answers to you. He perjured himself on the witness stand in a case you prosecuted."

She may not have recognized the man's face, but she knew the name—the name of the assistant district attorney. Could he have been the third man in the photograph—the one with his back to the camera? If so, then what she captured on film was even more damaging than they'd originally thought.

"You don't really think you can get away with this, do you, Lyle? You put me in prison for two years. Wasn't that enough? Why are you still after me?"

"Don't try to play me for a fool. You know this isn't about you." Lyle shot a quick glance in Brandi's direction. "It's about her and her photographs. I'm not sure how you got involved in this, but you sealed your fate when you did."

Reece stepped in front of Brandi, putting himself protectively between her and Lyle. "I'm not sure exactly what you're talking about or why strange things have been happening. For some reason Frank James has been stalking Miss Doyle, then he decided to abduct her. I've been trying to protect her from the lieutenant and figure out why he's doing this. Of course, I've known for a long time that Frank is a dirty cop. I just didn't know how high up it reached."

Lyle shook his head, his voice a combination of exasperation and irritation. "Knock it off. I'm not buying any of this *I don't know what's going on* line you're trying to hand me." He motioned with the shotgun, gesturing toward Reece's laptop computer. "I want that computer."

"My computer? There's nothing in it of interest to anyone but me. It's just a few games and the start of a novel I've been working on based on some of my past cases as a private investigator."

Lyle's features hardened into an angry mask. "I'm not playing games here. Give me the damn computer."

Reece slowly pulled the strap from over his head and held it out toward Lyle.

"Place it on the hood of your car, then step back."

He did as he was told, making sure that Brandi stayed behind him at all times. He toyed with the thought of telling Lyle about having sent copies of the photographs to a colleague out of state, but decided that it was better if Lyle didn't know there were any other loose ends. He needed to concentrate his efforts on getting out of the mess currently confronting him.

Several ideas darted through his mind, including simply rushing Lyle and tackling him before he could get off a shot. But Lyle had a shotgun, not a pistol. He didn't even need to have an accurate aim to stop both him and Brandi in their tracks. He needed to come up with something better, but what?

Then he felt her hand on his back.

Brandi steadied her trembling hand, then carefully raised the back of his sweatshirt just enough to get at his 9 mm pistol. Her heart pounded wildly, but she had total control of her actions. She removed the pistol from the holster and clicked off the safety. With Reece blocking Lyle's view of her, she knew she could do it without being seen. But now what? She had never fired that type of pistol and had certainly never shot at a person.

She took a calming breath. There wasn't time to debate the morality of it. The moment of truth had arrived. As the old cliché said, it was do or die. A combination of fear and panic surged through her body. A sick churning tried to work its way up her throat. She had never been so frightened in her entire life…a life that could be over any minute.

But if this was going to be how things ended, she knew what she had to say before it was too late. She leaned forward, her words a mere whisper, just loud enough for him to hear.

"In case we don't get out of this, I want you to know that I love you." She pressed against his side to let him know which way to move to clear a path for her shot.

She clenched her jaw into a hard line of determination. She had only a split second to make good on her shot. Her muscles tensed like a tightly coiled spring. She whispered the word to Reece, letting him know she was ready.

"Now."

He rushed into action, leaping in the direction she had indicated and drawing Lyle's attention away from her. She leveled the pistol at Lyle and squeezed off a shot. Lyle's cry of pain said she had made the shot good. Unfortunately, their adversary held on to his shotgun.

Lyle lurched to the side, seeking the protection of the carport wall. Reece turned to take the pistol from Brandi as he shoved her behind the SUV. Reece was out in the open—fair game for the shotgun. Before he could get himself to cover, Lyle stepped around the side of the carport with the shotgun leveled directly at him.

The sound of a shot exploded in the air.

Lyle dropped the shotgun and fell to the ground.

A moment of panic hit Reece as his gaze quickly swept the area looking for an explanation of what had happened. Then Joe Hodges appeared in his line of sight. Mixed feelings of shock and relief washed through him. He lowered the pistol and held out his hand toward Brandi to help her to her feet.

He watched as Joe kicked the shotgun out of Lyle's reach, then bent down to check his vital signs. When he was satisfied that Lyle had a strong enough pulse and a non-life-threatening wound, Joe searched him for additional weapons.

Then a flurry of activity seemed to erupt. The sound of a helicopter landing on the fire road. Frank James and another man, both in handcuffs, being escorted toward the cabin by two other men.

Joe communicated with the helicopter. "All three in custody, one injured. Come and get him. Transport to the emergency room, maintaining custody."

Reece pulled Brandi into his arms, holding her tightly in his embrace. "Are you all right?"

Her entire body trembled almost out of control. She slipped her arms around his waist and nestled her head against his shoulder. "Yes, I'm okay." She looked up at his face. "Is it really over?"

"Yes, it's finally over. You're safe now. They can't hurt you."

He continued to hold her, his cheek resting against the top of her head. It was so comforting being in his arms. She couldn't even describe what she felt other than completely drained. Her nerves and emotions had been in a constant state of turmoil for so long. It was a strange combination of elation, relief and confusion. Even the pouring rain couldn't dampen the emotions coursing through her.

Two more men arrived on the scene, apparently from the helicopter. They checked Lyle's vital signs, loaded him onto a stretcher and carried him back toward the fire road. A couple of minutes later he heard the helicopter take off. Then he heard more vehicles on the fire road. It sounded as if an entire assault force had been marshaled.

Joe turned his attention toward Reece and Brandi. Reece quickly holstered the 9 mm pistol, getting it out of sight.

"I don't know how you found me or why you're here, but I can't begin to tell you how glad I am to see you."

Joe ignored Reece's comment. "I believe we have some business to transact."

"Yes, we do." Reece retrieved his laptop computer from the hood of the SUV. "Let's go inside where it's dry and warm."

"You go ahead. I'll be there in a minute. I need to give some final instructions to my men."

Reece and Brandi headed for the front door of the cabin. He glanced back over his shoulder and watched for a couple of seconds as Joe spoke to his team, then they led Frank and the other man away. Joe had a quick conversation with another of his agents, then everyone except Joe and one of his men disappeared from sight.

Reece ushered Brandi inside and closed the door. He pulled her into his arms again, then brushed a tender kiss across her lips. "We definitely have things to talk about now. Your words…what you said—"

"Okay, Reece. Let's have everything."

The opening of the door and Joe's voice interrupted Reece. He quickly turned Brandi loose.

They spent the next half hour with Reece showing all the items to Joe and explaining everything he hadn't already told him.

"And what about that pistol you had?"

Reece cocked his head and raised a questioning eyebrow. "Pistol? What pistol? I'm not allowed to have any firearms, at least not until I get my conviction overturned."

Brandi's words cut into their conversation. "The pistol was mine. I've had it for a long time. I freely admit that it's not registered, but I don't carry it as a concealed weapon either. I kept it at my house. I retrieved it that first night when we went to my house to try and figure out what was missing."

Joe shot her with a look that said he didn't believe a word she was saying. She held her breath, waiting for his response. After what seemed like an eternity, he wrote the information in his notebook.

"Well, I guess that will explain the bullets from two different weapons."

A furtive glance passed between Brandi and Reece, followed by a look of relief that Joe had decided not to press the matter.

A hint of nervousness continued to cling to Reece's voice. "Now that we've answered your questions and turned over all the evidence, perhaps you could answer a few questions for me."

Joe closed his notebook. "What do you want to know?"

Reece's tone of voice conveyed several questions all wrapped up in one. "What the hell were you doing here?"

"Trying to keep you from totally blowing my investigation out of the water."

"Me? What investigation?"

"For the last year I've been involved in an investigation of organized crime infiltrating local political offices and law enforcement agencies. I've had Lyle Hanover and Frank James in my sights for six months. And then you walked into the middle of it. I wasn't sure what to do, especially with you playing it so cagey and not confiding anything other than Frank James's name. But as soon as I heard your story I knew you were in the middle of a lot more than you realized."

"A little word of warning from you wouldn't have hurt."

"You know better than that. I couldn't divulge any information about an ongoing investigation."

"How did you find this cabin, and why were you here when we were supposed to be meeting elsewhere?"

"I had a team of people working on finding you. We finally came across the utilities and property title in your mother's maiden name. Then when I got a list of what you purchased from the electronics supply store—fortunately you didn't find the second tracking bug before that stop—I knew you were gearing up for some trouble. I put Frank and Lyle under surveillance and came out here myself at night to look at this location."

"So that was you who set off the monitor alarm. Got out of the car, looked around, pointed to something, then got in your car and drove away."

"As soon as the surveillance reported that Frank and Lyle were together with a third man and headed in this direction, I knew where they were going. We beat them here and staked out your cabin. And the rest you know."

"I guess that covers everything. Well, *almost* everything. There is something you can do for me in exchange for the proof you needed showing the organized crime connection."

"And what would that be?"

"You could put in a good word along with an official written report to the governor saying why I should have my conviction overturned and my private investigator's license restored."

"Simple enough. Consider it done."

"Thanks." Reece glanced at Brandi, then returned his attention to Joe. "Are we through here? I have some important unfinished business I need to take care of."

Joe rose from his chair. "Yes, we're through here for the time being. I'll need to have both of you come to my office so we can do an official report and discuss what part the two of you will play in the subsequent proceedings. Will ten o'clock Monday morning be convenient?"

Reece shot a questioning look in Brandi's direction and she nodded her agreement. He turned toward Joe. "That will be fine. See you then."

It only took a few more minutes to wrap up everything. Joe Hodges and the other FBI agent left. Reece closed the door, then turned toward Brandi.

"Alone at last. We need to talk."

"Yes, I suppose we do." A thousand butterflies

collided inside her stomach. Had she made a colossal mistake when she'd told him she loved him? Was he looking for some way to let her down easy? Was she about to face a second moment of truth in one day? First the showdown with Frank James and his cohorts—ending in her actually shooting a man—and now this?

He grabbed her hand and led her over to the sofa. After building a fire, he sat next to her. He pulled her to him, then placed a loving kiss on her lips. A low-level uneasy hum ran through his body. He knew what he wanted to say, but didn't know how to say it.

He nervously cleared his throat. "You can't begin to imagine how much your words touched me. I only hope you really meant them rather than saying them in a moment of emotional turmoil." He shifted his weight and turned until he faced her. "I love you, Brandi. I truly do. Until now I haven't had anything to offer you other than my love. I had a prison record and an uncertain future, not terrific things to bring to a relationship. But now the circumstances have changed. I should be able to get my conviction overturned and my career restored. We have a future and I want us to spend it together."

"Oh, Reece..." She threw her arms around his neck. Tears of joy welled in her eyes. "I love you. I really do. I meant every word."

"I know we've only known each other a week, but it's been quite the week. Is it too soon to ask you to marry me?"

"It's not too soon at all. And my answer is yes."

* * * * *

Turn the page for a sneak preview of
IF I'D NEVER KNOWN YOUR LOVE
by
Georgia Bockoven

From the brand-new series
Harlequin Everlasting Love
Every great love has a story to tell.™

One year, five months and four days missing

There's no way for you to know this, Evan, but I haven't written to you for a few months. Actually, it's been almost a year. I had a hard time picking up a pen once more after we paid the second ransom and then received a letter saying it wasn't enough. I was so sure you were coming home that I took the kids along to Bogotá so they could fly home with you and me, something I swore I'd never do. I've fallen in love with Colombia and the people who've opened their hearts to me. But fear is a constant companion when I'm there. I won't ever expose our children to that kind of danger again.

I'm at a loss over what to do anymore, Evan. I've begged and pleaded and thrown temper tantrums with every official I can corner both here and at home. They've been incredibly tolerant and understanding, but in the end as ineffectual as the rest of us.

I try to imagine what your life is like now, what you do every day, what you're wearing, what you eat. I want to believe that the people who have you are misguided yet kind, that they treat you well. It's how I survive day to day. To think of you being mistreated hurts too much. If I picture you locked away somewhere and suffering, a weight descends on me that makes it almost impossible to get out of bed in the morning.

Your captors surely know you by now. They have to recognize what a good man you are. I imagine you working with their children, telling them that you have children, too, showing them the pictures you carry in your wallet. Can't the men who have you understand how much your children miss you? How can it not matter to them?

How can they keep you away from us all this time? Over and over, we've done what they asked. Are they oblivious to the depth of their cruelty? What kind of people are they that they don't care?

I used to keep a calendar beside our bed next to the peach rose you picked for me before you left. Every night I marked another day, counting how many you'd been gone. I don't do that any longer. I don't want to be reminded of all the days we'll never get back.

When I can't sleep at night, I tell you about my day. I imagine you hearing me and smiling over the details that make up my life now. I never tell you how defeated I feel at moments or how hard I work to hide it from everyone for fear they will see it as a reason to stop believing you are coming home to us.

And I couldn't tell you about the lump I found in my breast and how difficult it was going through all the tests without you here to lean on. The lump was benign—the process reaching that diagnosis utterly terrifying. I couldn't stop thinking about what would happen to Shelly and Jason if something happened to me.

We need you to come home.

I'm worn down with missing you.

I'm going to read this tomorrow and will probably tear it up or burn it in the fireplace. I don't want you to get the idea I ever doubted what I was doing to free you or thought the work a burden. I would gladly spend the rest of my life at it, even if, in the end, we only had one day together.

You are my life, Evan.

I will love you forever.

* * * * *

Don't miss this deeply moving
Harlequin Everlasting Love
story about a woman's struggle to bring back her
kidnapped husband from Colombia
and her turmoil over whether to let go,
finally, and welcome another man into her life.
IF I'D NEVER KNOWN YOUR LOVE
by Georgia Bockoven
is available March 27, 2007.

And also look for
THE NIGHT WE MET
by Tara Taylor Quinn,
a story about finding love
when you least expect it.

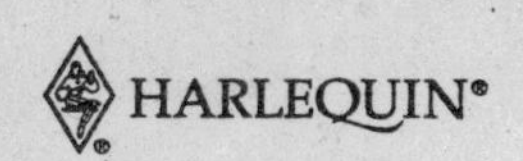

INTRIGUE®

COMING NEXT MONTH

#981 SPECIAL ASSIGNMENT by Ann Voss Peterson
Bodyguards Unlimited, Denver, CO (Book 2 of 6)
Mike Lawson is just the type of honest cop needed to protect Prescott agent Cassie Allen as police corruption overruns Denver.

#982 PRESCRIPTION: MAKEOVER by Jessica Andersen
In order to expose a vast conspiracy, Ike Rombout undergoes a full makeover that turns her into exactly the sort of girly-girl she despises—only to catch the watchful eye of investigator William Caine.

#983 A SOLDIER'S OATH by Debra Webb
Colby Agency: The Equalizers (Book 1 of 3)
Spencer Anders joined the Equalizers to start over. But can he recover Willow Harris's son from the Middle East *and* give Willow a chance at a new beginning?

#984 COMPROMISED SECURITY by Cassie Miles
Safe House: Mesa Verde (Book 2 of 2)
FBI special agents Flynn O'Conner and Marisa Kelso must confront their darkest, most personal secrets while pursuing an elusive killer.

#985 SECRET CONTRACT by Dana Marton
Mission: Redemption (Book 1 of 4)
Undercover soldier Nick Tarasov has been after an untouchable arms dealer for years, but this time he has Carly Jones with him—and she has nothing to lose.

#986 FINDING HIS CHILD by Tracy Montoya
Search-and-rescue tracker Sabrina Adelante never gave up looking for Aaron Donovan's daughter. Aaron still believes his daughter is out along Renegade Ridge, but is he seeking closure—or vengeance?

www.eHarlequin.com

HICNM0307